'You Have Bedroom Hair.'

'Excuse me?' Windy asked, surprised.

'Your hair looks like you just tumbled out of bed.' Sky wiggled his eyebrows. 'Nothing's sexier than a thoroughly loved woman with tangled hair.'

For Pete's sake. What a thing for him to say, especially after she'd been fantasising about sleeping in his arms. 'My hair always looks like this.' And she'd never been thoroughly loved. Windy tried not to blush.

She knew her lack of experience was showing. Although plenty of men found her attractive, she'd never lost her heart, made earth-shattering love or even cuddled in masculine arms all night. Call her old-fashioned, but she didn't mind waiting for the real thing.

Sky clanked a spoon against his cup. With a start, Windy looked up to find him watching her, a knowing look in his eye.

Dear Reader,

Welcome to Desire™, the series guaranteed to bring you powerful, passionate and provocative love stories!

This month we have excitement and glamour in the latest instalment of ROYALLY WED, Anne Marie Winston's *The Pregnant Princess*. ROYALLY WED continues next month in Special Edition with Joan Elliott Pickart's *Man…Mercenary…Monarch*, the long-lost brother's story.

Our MAN OF THE MONTH is Tanner Bennett, the sexy hero of Cait London's *Last Dance*: Tanner's determined to woo his wife back into his arms! And there's a compelling tale of a marriage of convenience in Cathleen Galitz's *The Cowboy Takes a Bride*, this month's THE BRIDAL BID book.

In fabulous Elizabeth Bevarly's *Dr Mummy* a couple are reunited by a baby left on a doorstep, and Sheri WhiteFeather returns with another sexy Native American hero in *Skyler Hawk: Lone Brave*. Finally, in BJ James's latest BLACK WATCH book, *Night Music*, two wounded souls discover the healing power of love!

Enjoy them all,

The Editors

Skyler Hawk:
Lone Brave

SHERI
WHITEFEATHER

™SILHOUETTE
DESIRE®

*Silhouette, Silhouette Desire and Colophon
are registered trademarks of Harlequin Books S.A.,
used under licence.*

*First published in Great Britain 2001
Silhouette Books, Eton House, 18-24 Paradise Road,
Richmond, Surrey TW9 1SR*

© Sheree Henry-WhiteFeather 2000

ISBN 0 373 76272 0

22-0201

*Printed and bound in Spain
by Litografia Rosés S.A., Barcelona*

SHERI WHITEFEATHER

lives in Southern California and enjoys ethnic dining, summer powwows and visiting art galleries and vintage clothing shops near the beach. Since her one true passion is writing, she is thrilled to be a part of the Silhouette Desire® line. When she isn't writing, she often reads until the wee hours of the morning.

Sheri also works as a leather artisan with her Native American husband, Dru. They have one son and a menagerie of pets, including a pampered English bulldog and four equally spoiled Bengal cats. She would love to hear from her readers. You may write to her at: P.O. Box 5130, Orange, California 92863-5130, USA.

To my husband, Dru, for teaching me to appreciate all of God's creatures, including the ones that slither.
To Raven, for letting me borrow your son.
And to my own son, Nikki—you'll always be my baby, no matter how big you get.

One

A nice, quiet young man?

Tall, dark and gorgeous would have been more accurate. Windy Hall gazed at the stranger standing on the other side of her front door. Edith Burke, her elderly landlady, had described him as a "nice, quiet young man." So upon Edith's recommendation, Windy had agreed, sight unseen, to share her two-bedroom rental with him, at least temporarily.

Maybe she had mistaken this man for her new roommate. Maybe he was selling something or collecting for a charity. Yeah, right. Hunks of America. "You aren't Skyler Reed by any chance, are you?"

"Sure am." He flashed a slightly crooked smile complete with a set of twin dimples. "But just Sky will do."

Okay, no mistake. She extended her hand. "Nice to meet you. I'm Windy."

"Hello, Windy." As he clasped her hand, he spoke her name in a husky baritone. "The pleasure's mine."

A pair of dark sunglasses and shoulder-length black hair

gave Sky Reed a renegade appeal, clearly contradicting the boyish dimples. A white T-shirt clung to his chest, then tapered into the waistband of well-worn jeans, emphasizing a lean yet muscular physique. Copper skin and razor-edged cheekbones boasted a Native American heritage, whereas his towering height, flared nostrils and square jaw hinted at European ancestry. Since Edith had said he worked with horses, the Western drawl and dusty cowboy boots were no surprise.

But the flirtatious grin, Windy decided, was anybody's guess. She withdrew her hand from his grasp and fingered the hem on her T-shirt. Even his handshake sizzled with sexuality. Lord, what had she gotten herself into?

Act normal. Don't let his *looks* fluster you. It's a man's heart that counts. "Come in. I'll show you around so you can get settled."

Sky pushed his sunglasses onto his head. "Thanks, but I'm not officially moving in until tonight. I'm on my way to work and thought I oughta stop by and meet you first."

Windy started to respond, but upon seeing his eyes, found herself immobilized. And mute.

Blue. His eyes were blue—clear and vibrant, sparkling against that bronzed complexion and shock of black hair. The exotic combination weakened her knees. But before they could buckle, she decided his cerulean gaze was just an illusion—tinted contacts. Mixed genetics or not, no one that dark had eyes that blue.

His voice jarred her back to the subject at hand. "Edith said you had the extra house key."

"Oh, of course. I'll get it for you."

Sky followed her into the living room then scanned the surroundings.

"It's still a little barren," Windy said. No knickknacks, no pictures on the walls, no stereo, no TV. "I wasn't robbed. I was vandalized. Most of my belongings were broken."

The horrifying experience had left her feeling violated and afraid. "My last roommate moved out a week before it happened. We weren't getting along very well because she hadn't paid her share of the rent for two months, but the police said she was not involved. This wasn't a lone incident. Some other houses in the neighborhood were hit.'' All of them had females living there. Young, single women.

''Yeah, Edith told me all about it. They won't come back. Not with me staying here.''

That's why she had agreed to allow a man to move in—a man her landlady trusted implicitly. And why wouldn't Edith trust Sky? According to the elderly woman, Sky had saved her life—pushed her to safety before a drunk driver could run her over. That made him special in Windy's eyes, too. Although Sky would only be in town for three months, she hoped by the time he moved out the vandals would have forgotten about her.

''At least they didn't destroy my furniture. There are a few nicks in the coffee table, but other than that everything is okay.''

Sky nodded, and Windy wondered if he approved of her taste. She had decorated with inexpensive yet trendy furnishings: a black leather sofa, a matching recliner, a colorful area rug. She liked the idea of placing modern furniture in an old house, contrasting with the hardwood floors and paned windows, especially since they expressed their own brand of charm.

''Since I travel so often, I don't have much to contribute,'' he said. ''But I do have a TV and a stereo. I reckon that'll help some.''

Windy accepted his offer along with his goodhearted bad-boy smile. ''Helps a lot. There's so much to replace. I still haven't restocked my dishes.'' The vandals had left the kitchen floor covered with broken glass and chips of her mother's china. The sight had evoked a torrent of tears. She considered her mother's hand-painted china a family heirloom. It had been a link to her childhood, to home-cooked meals and holidays gone by. Windy had lost her bright-spirited mother two years before, and the shattered dishes had snapped the last of her threadbare emotions. But thanks to Edith Burke, she had survived that awful day. Although Edith had lent a sympathetic ear, the older woman gently affirmed that Windy's mind hadn't been vandalized, and with or without the china, she still owned a lifetime of precious memories.

Sky leaned against the empty entertainment center. "I really appreciate you letting me bunk here. Edith told me you were a sweet little filly. Pretty, too."

Windy stifled a giggle. She knew the retired schoolteacher hadn't described her as a little filly. Sweet and pretty, maybe. A petite young lady, definitely. But being typecast didn't bother Windy. She considered herself attractive and likable. The girl next door, with a hair disorder: her stubborn, blond hair hung down her back in its usual, unmanageable waves.

"Edith said nice things about you, too." However, the elderly woman had neglected to mention his charming grin. Or his sapphire gaze. As usual, Windy's curious nature took over. "I couldn't help but notice your eyes. Tinted lenses, right?"

He chuckled, making her realize she wasn't the first to ask.

"No, honey, they're mine. I wouldn't do this on purpose."

Do what? Make himself even more handsome? Her knees threatened to buckle again. "My God, they're beautiful."

"Thanks."

Although he shrugged indifferently, she sensed embarrassment in the gesture. As an awkward vibration silenced them, she twisted a strand of her unruly mane. Skyler Reed with the sky-blue eyes. A striking name for a striking man. No illusion there.

"The extra key is in the kitchen," she said, inviting him to follow her once again.

The kitchen decor included a scarred wood table, limited counter space and a stainless-steel sink. Gingham curtains and a ladybug border added accents of red.

Straining on her toes, she located the key on the top shelf of the pantry, then sent it clanking to the tiled floor.

"Oh, shoot. I'll get—"

"No, let me."

They lunged at the same time and, amid the checkerboard gingham and fluttering ladybugs, they collided.

Windy lost her balance from the force but, instead of landing in an ungraceful heap, Sky caught her in his arms.

Windy's heart jolted, her pulse pounding as he brushed a wisp of hair from her cheek.

"Are you okay?" he asked, tossing her that slow, crooked smile.

"Yes," she answered, her body warming. He smelled of male spice: leather, denim and musk. A forbidden attraction sizzled through her veins. Without thinking, she moved closer, brushing the heat of his skin. An erratic breath rushed through her lungs. Good God, what was happening to her?

Sky's jaw turned taut. A muscle in his cheek twitched. He handled her gently, as though she were a kitten. He stroked her back, then slid his hands down her spine, chasing the chills he'd created. But an instant later he seemed confused, as if trying to remember how she had ended up in his arms.

"The key." He dropped his hands and scanned the floor. "Where's the key?"

As casually as possible Windy eased away from him. "I don't know." She glanced down at the empty space below her feet. "It was right here."

Avoiding eye contact, they both examined the gray-and-white pattern on the tile, the dust on his boots, tan laces on her shoes.

"There!" Windy pointed to the speck of gold glittering beneath the refrigerator door.

"I'll get it." He scooped up the key and jammed it into his pocket. "We must have…um…kicked it or something."

She took a deep breath. Okay, so they'd stumbled into an accidental hug. No big deal. It was over. It wouldn't happen again. "Where do you work?" she asked, desperate for something to say.

He braced his shoulder against the refrigerator. "Rodeo Knights."

"The place with those Wild West acts?" She'd heard of

it—a horse theater featuring matinee and evening shows with cowboys, Indians, and a barbecued meal. "What do you do?"

"Ya know, trick riding. Some stunts."

"Wow." So the man was a daredevil. "Edith just said you worked with horses, but she didn't specify how exactly."

"Been a trick rider most of my life. The guy who owns the theater is an old friend. An old boss, really. We were a specialty act on the rodeo circuit until he opened Rodeo Knights."

"How come your job isn't permanent?" When he raised an eyebrow at her question, she brought her landlady back into the conversation. "Edith said you'd only be in town for the summer."

Hunching his shoulders, he hooked his thumbs into his front pockets. "Don't wanna stay. I mean, hell, California? Three months is about all I can take. Why Charlie picked L.A. to settle down in is beyond me."

She assumed Charlie was his boss. "Burbank is the perfect town for a Western theater." Windy knew Rodeo Knights was located between the Media District and the Equestrian Center. "I hear it's doing well."

"Yeah. Charlie thinks he's gonna con me into staying longer, but it'll never happen."

Windy decided not to take offense, even if California was her home state. "I grew up here. Edith was my sixth-grade teacher. Sometimes it seems strange not to call her Mrs. Burke."

He grinned. "Yeah, she told me you were one of her students. She also said you were a teacher now."

Windy nodded. "Preschool."

The grin faded. "You work with little kids?"

Why the distressed look? Was he worried she might bring a toddler home? "Don't you like small children?"

His nonchalant shrug mocked the twitch in his jaw. "Don't know any. Charlie has a daughter, but she's older."

Did he like Charlie's daughter? "How old?"

"Twelve."

She assumed from his simple response that he wasn't interested in offering more information than he'd been asked to give. Windy didn't mind expressing herself. She could turn small talk into important issues. "I love children, all ages, but teaching preschool isn't my lifelong goal. I'm a psychology major. Someday I intend to make a difference. There are too many dysfunctional families out there."

Although Sky smiled once again, his sparkling gaze had dimmed considerably. "That's great that you're following your dream, but this conversation's gettin' too deep for me. I'm a single guy. What do I know about dysfunctional families?"

Judging from the forced smile, plenty, she thought. The analyst in Windy snapped to attention. Taking a step back, she studied his features, then let her gaze assess his body language: a vacant stare; a twitching jaw; long, tanned fingers opening then closing into tight fists. Broad-shouldered yet vulnerable, with a smile far too lonely. Even his dimples were hiding.

Maybe the traveling cowboy wasn't a drifter. Maybe he was running from his past. Running and afraid to look back. Suddenly his unlikely alliance with their elderly landlady puzzled her. How did the older woman and the dashing young cowboy come to be friends? And why were they together when that drunk driver skidded onto the sidewalk? Where were they going?

"How did you and Edith meet?" she asked.

Sky pulled the house key from his pocket, ran his fingers over the serrated edge. "Didn't she tell you about the accident?"

"You mean that's how you met? You were strangers on the same street corner? I assumed you were friends already."

"Really?" He shifted his booted feet, jammed the key back into his pocket. "And here I'd thought Edith told you about—" He swallowed and glanced away. "That car hit me."

Windy pressed a hand to her heart. "Oh, my God. Were you hurt?"

"Yeah…I…" He tugged a hand through his hair, then met

her concerned gaze with a wary one. "I'd really prefer you talk to Edith about this. Besides, I should check out my room and get going. Charlie's expecting me."

Windy didn't know how to respond, or how to feel. Unfortunately, she hadn't asked Edith about Sky's background. Although she had found herself impressed by his heroic deed, Edith's description of the "nice young man," had made him sound boring. Average. Yet the man standing across from her was far from ordinary. Not only had he saved someone's life, he'd been injured in the process.

She smiled, hoping to put him at ease. Apparently he wasn't comfortable discussing the accident.

"Your room is the second door on the right. The bed was delivered yesterday." Windy knew Sky had called ahead and asked their landlady to rent him some furnishings—the landlady Windy intended to call for some answers.

Sky decided not to go home after work. At least not right away. But unfortunately, the loud, crowded bar was no consolation. He couldn't stop thinking about his new roommate.

He reached for his jacket, then fingered the cigarettes in the front pocket. He'd quit smoking months ago, but keeping a pack handy kept the cravings in check. Sky knew he had an I-always-want-what-I-can't-have personality. So with that in mind, he'd made sure forbidden pleasures weren't too much of a temptation. And that's why he had agreed to bunk with a woman—a pretty one. Meaningless sex was off-limits, too.

"Can I get you another drink?" The cocktail waitress smiled. Leggy and lean in a short red dress, she tossed a dark wave of hair over her shoulder.

He glanced down at the glass bottle. How long had he been nursing the same beer? "No, thanks, I'm fine," he answered, conscious of the brunette's body language. There was a day when he would have responded to her subtle flirtation. She was attractive, in a hard sort of way. Things like that never mattered much in the past. He would have taken her home, anyway. Another nameless, faceless woman. Another loveless sexual encounter. Loneliness.

What the hell was he doing? Trying to cool the heat he felt for his new roommate with a drink? After ten minutes they had ended up in each other's arms. But instead of letting Windy go, he'd caressed her, held her close and enjoyed the feel of her slender body, sensual scent of her perfume. The woman smelled like his favorite dessert—her vanilla scent reminding him of ice cream melting over smooth, warm flesh.

Boy, some hero he turned out to be. Edith had asked him to protect Windy from vandals, not seduce her in the kitchen. Sky had expected her to be cute, but not sexy and innocent wrapped in one curvaceous little package. Although he used to bed a variety of women, he favored the tall sultry type, so Edith's description of his future roommate seemed like a mild temptation. Petite and pretty, the old lady had said.

Try angelic. Sweet. Sensual. A breezy smile, honest eyes and long, stormy blond hair. The name Windy suited her well. Just thinking about her played havoc with his already frazzled emotions. Not to mention his eight-month bout with celibacy.

Sky tasted the imported beer and winced. Practically warm now. He motioned to the waitress, then slid the offending bottle away. "I think I will take a fresh one, honey."

"Sure." As she reached for the half-empty bottle, her bodice brushed his shoulder. His mind on another woman, he ignored the contact.

What would Windy think of him if she knew the truth? Would she have welcomed him into her home? Sky shook his head, an agitated frown furrowing his brow. Not likely. Sure, Edith would fill her in about the accident, but the old lady would make him sound like a modern-day Sir Lancelot rather than a no-good cowboy with amnesia—a man who wasn't even sure about his own last name. Then again, Edith didn't know the whole story. She didn't know about things he actually did remember.

Within five minutes the leggy brunette returned. "Here you go." She set the beer on the table, took his money, thanked him for the tip, then appeared to notice his frown. "I've never seen you here before," she said. "Are you new in town?"

"Yeah." He glanced at the lime wedge floating in his beer. "I'm movin' in with a girl."

"She the reason you're scowling?"

He laughed. Perceptive woman. "Yeah."

Apparently not the type to go after someone else's man, she offered some advice, "Maybe you should go home and apologize."

Sky leaned back in the chair. The waitress thought he had a live-in lover. That would be the day. "What makes you think I owe her an apology?"

She tapped a candy-apple-red fingernail on the table. "You look guilty."

Guilty. Hell, no woman ever made him guilty. He didn't stick around long enough to feel anything. "Whatever," he said, wanting the cocktail waitress to leave him alone.

Okay, maybe he did feel guilty, but it wasn't Windy he owed an apology to. It was that little boy who deserved an explanation—the little boy crowding his jumbled memories. His son. The child Skyler had wronged.

Windy lounged in bed, phone in hand, dialing Edith's number. Although this was her third attempt to reach the woman, leaving a message wasn't possible. Edith Burke didn't own an answering machine.

When a familiar voice answered, she pitched forward. "Hi, Edith. This is Windy. I'm sorry for calling so late, but I couldn't reach you earlier."

"Oh, hello, dear. I was at the homeless shelter. You know I volunteer every Friday."

Suddenly guilty, Windy took a bite of the takeout meal she'd ordered. While the elderly woman had spent her evening feeding the homeless, Windy had painted her toenails and nibbled on a carton of Chinese stir-fry. "I met Sky. He's moving in tonight."

"Isn't he a nice young man?"

"Seems to be." She stabbed a mushroom with the plastic fork. "Although he's not what I expected."

Edith cleared her throat. "I suppose I should have warned you about his grammar. I don't let him curse around me, and you shouldn't, either. If it bothers you, I'll speak to him about it."

Windy wasn't about to correct a man like Sky about his dialect. She could live with his misuse of the English language. And an occasional hell and damn never hurt anyone.

"That won't be necessary. He was a perfect gentleman." And I was a perfect lady. Sort of. I dropped the house key and we ended up in each other's arms. Of course, now I can't stop thinking about him. "Sky looks different than I thought he would."

Edith responded in her typical no-nonsense fashion. "I didn't mention how handsome he was because I didn't want you to think I was trying to be a matchmaker. You know I'm not encouraging hanky-panky. Sky knows that, as well." The elderly woman continued in a softer voice. "But you don't have to worry about him. Sky is a decent man. He would never take advantage of a lady."

Not unless she wanted to be taken advantage of, Windy thought. Sky might be decent, but he wasn't exactly Boy Scout material. Nor would he be canonized a saint. That smile bordered on devilish.

Edith cleared her throat again and Windy adjusted the phone, anxious for some answers. "Why didn't you tell me he was hit by that car?"

The other woman sighed. "I thought it was Sky's place to tell you."

"Why? What happened to him?"

"Oh, goodness. I should have known he wouldn't tell you all of it."

Windy grimaced. "All of what?"

Edith sighed again. "Sky lost his memory in the accident. He remembers very little about himself."

Windy's heartbeat doubled. Amnesia? Sky had amnesia?

"Oh, my God." No wonder he had a difficult time talking about the accident. "He must remember something. I get the feeling he's at odds with his past."

The other end of the line remained silent, as though Edith pondered Windy's observation. When she finally answered, her voice lowered. "There is a bit more to his story, but it's much too complicated to discuss over the phone. I promise we'll get together this week. We'll have a cup of tea, and I'll tell you everything I know."

Anxious, she toyed with her fork. "I don't think I can wait that long."

Edith "tsked" like a disapproving grandmother. "You always were an impatient one. A few days won't make a difference to you or to Sky. That accident happened almost sixteen years ago." Fatigue sounded in the older woman's voice. "Now I should get to bed. It's late and I have a busy day tomorrow."

Windy knew Edith's days consisted of volunteer work: church rummage sales, women's shelters, literacy tutoring. Things far more important than Windy's nagging curiosity. "Okay. I'll see you soon."

"Goodbye, dear."

Windy tossed the phone aside and filled her mouth with another bite just as a light knock vibrated her bedroom door.

"Honey, it's Sky."

Honey? The endearment sounded intimate—sensuous and husky—even through the thick, painted wood. The food nearly stuck in her throat. "Just a minute," she called back.

She bounded off the bed. Should she open the door and peek out the crack, or keep it closed and simply ask what he wanted?

No. She smoothed her oversize attire. That would seem rude. Smile and act friendly. Platonic friendly, she reminded herself. Don't pant or drool. And don't pester him about his memory. Be patient. Professional.

She opened the door just enough to expose her head and shoulders. "Hi."

"Hi." A slow smile spread across his face. "I saw your light on. I hope I'm not disturbing you."

"No. I'm up." And breathing him in. She tried not to, but couldn't help herself. His scent had changed. An earthy blend misted him now. Horses, hay and…beer?

She looked into his eyes. A gaze as clear and blue as a summer sea stared back at her. A social drink, she decided. He wasn't drunk.

"Just wanted to let you know that I'm movin' my things in," he said. "Didn't want the noise to scare you."

"Okay. Thanks." Windy noticed he wore the same clothes, but his hair wasn't flowing over his shoulders. It rested in a tight ponytail at his nape. "How was work?"

"Good. It was my first day, but I know the routine."

"Did you work the early show?"

"Yeah."

She wanted to touch his dimples. He looked boyish when he smiled, rugged when he didn't. "Do you play a cowboy or an Indian?"

"Both." The left dimple indented deeper than the right. "In one segment I'm an Indian. In the other, a villainous cowboy. I get shot in that one. Fall right off my horse." Shyness crept into his voice. "And then near the end, I'm just me. Riding and roping."

"Do you like being a performer?" Unlike most of the gorgeous L.A. population, Sky didn't fit the let's-have-lunch, I-want-to-be-a-star mold. But then, how could he? He hated California.

He shrugged. "The horses are the true performers. I just consider myself along for the ride."

A fast, crazy ride, no doubt.

Windy realized she had allowed the door to fall open while they'd chatted. She stood in full view now. A tousled blonde in a Minnie Mouse nightshirt and bare feet, an unmade bed and carton of half-eaten stir-fry behind her. She sent him a nervous smile. Her room had caught his attention. She could see him scouring it with an amused gaze. Apparently he hadn't

expected mosquito netting and various shades of leopard and
zebra prints.

"My room wasn't vandalized," she said. "I guess they
didn't get that far." Thank God. Although she didn't keep
anything particularly valuable in her bedroom, it was her sanctuary, with her bras and panties, scented candles and perfumes.

"I like the jungle motif. Always thought animal prints were
sexy."

"Oh, umm…thanks." She glanced back at the bed. It did
look sexy. Wild and inviting. What a thing for him to notice.

Silence clung to the air like moss. Thick and heady.

When he shifted his stance, his boots scraped the hardwood
floor. "Guess I should bring my stuff in. The terrarium won't
fit in my bedroom, though. It'll have to go in the living room."

Terrarium, aquarium. Plants, fish. It didn't matter. She
needed to escape. He stood too close, smelled too virile,
looked too good. "That's fine. Good night, Sky."

"'Night, Pretty Windy."

Pretty Windy. She closed the door and leaned against it.
Another minute and she would have melted into a pool of hot,
steaming liquid.

Oh, get over it, she told herself, hating the watery feeling
in her legs. Swooning over a man was shallow and immature.
She knew better. Dang it. What was it about him that had her
behaving like a doe-eyed teenager? The cowboy drawl and
long-legged swagger? The shoulder-length hair and sparkling
blue eyes? Or was she just caught up in the mystery surrounding him?

Moving toward the bed, Windy fingered the sheets. She
knew. Deep down, she knew. Troubled souls fascinated her.
And this troubled soul sported dimples and a crooked smile.
A dangerous combination for a woman hell-bent on mending
fractured lives.

She sighed and climbed under the covers, even though sleep
would be a long time coming.

The following morning brought a bright ray of sunshine and
a stiff neck. Windy stretched and groaned. What her weary

body needed was a long luxurious shower, water therapy. After gathering a fluffy new bath towel and her favorite worn-out terry cloth robe, she stumbled down the hall to the bathroom, noting Sky's door remained closed.

A pulsating spray from the shower head massaged her shoulders, washing away the tension. She hadn't slept well. Her "sexy" bed, with its sleek leopard-print quilt, had blanketed her like a jungle cat's warm, muscular body—a jungle cat with exotic blue eyes.

Struggling to clear her mind, Windy reached for the shampoo, squeezed a large citrus-scented dollop into her hands and lathered her hair. Don't think about him, she told herself. Don't think about his lopsided grin or his—

Something brushed her foot. She glanced down. Something long and gray.

A snake!

She froze, praying sleep deprivation had fueled her imagination. But when she glanced down again, it was still there. A huge slithering creature, coiling in the splash of water.

Windy screamed, then jumped, her feet slipping and sliding on the slick white porcelain. Suds stinging her eyes, she climbed out of the tub. Still shrieking in blind panic, she snatched her robe and raced out the door.

In the hallway she fumbled with the robe as her legs turned rubbery. Oh no! Not her robe. A towel. A lousy towel, which of course meant her robe was somewhere in the bathroom. With an enormous snake.

Shivering, Windy wrapped the towel around herself. What if that reptile was a rattler or a man-eating python? She'd heard stories on the news—snakes who'd attempted to eat people, swallowing their limbs whole.

Modesty be damned. She clutched the towel and headed straight for Sky's room.

Two

"Skyyyy!"

He shot straight up from a deep sleep, blinking and squinting, trying to focus on the frantic woman screaming in his bedroom. Instantly he panicked.

"Is the house on fire?"

"No!" Windy pranced around nervously. "There's a snake in the bathtub! A snake!"

Relieved, he sighed, then fell back onto the bed, his rapid heartbeat stabilizing. "It's okay, honey, that's just Tequila. She won't hurt you."

"Tequila?" Her mouth fell open. "You mean that thing is some sort of pet? That horrid, slimy thing?"

Sky sat up, pushed several stray hairs away from his face and evaluated Windy with an irritated frown. Tequila wasn't a "thing."

A moment later he found himself amused. There she was, dancing around, dripping water onto the hardwood floor, while struggling to keep the towel on with one hand and wiping shampoo suds off her forehead with the other. He bit down on his bottom lip to suppress laughter and watched her bat away another stream of suds. He almost felt sorry for her. Almost. The woman had insulted Tequila.

"Dang you, Sky," she shrieked. "I can't believe you brought a snake into this house. A *snake*. My God, that thing is as big as me. I could have had a heart attack."

"I told you last night I was puttin' her terrarium in the living room."

"I thought you were talking about a plant terrarium. Or a fish aquarium." She narrowed her watery eyes. "If I had known you meant a snake…oh…just get that thing out of the bathroom."

"All right. Calm down, okay?" He slid out of bed and strode past her, reaching for the front tie on his low-riding shorts. What a way to begin the day—his gray sweat shorts nearly falling off his hips while his sexy roommate stood wrapped in a towel.

The bathroom check proved futile. He turned off the water, grabbed Windy's robe and returned to find her hopping up and down, alternating feet. He withheld a grin. Did she think the snake would bite her toes?

"Tequila's not in the bathroom. At least not that I could see, but there was a hole in one of the cabinets." A hole leading to the wall interior, he'd noticed. "I can't patch it till I find her, though. She might have slipped through it."

Windy's sniffling grew louder, warning the threat of tears. "What am I going to do?"

Aw shoot, Sky thought, she was gonna cry. He held out her robe and turned away, even though he would have enjoyed watching her towel fall. Watery eyes and soapy hair didn't detract from Windy's figure. Although her legs weren't long, they boasted a slender shape, with just the right amount of muscle tone. Sky glanced up at the beamed ceiling, deciding it best not to envision her breasts swelling beneath that flowery-printed towel. Having her in his room proved difficult enough. She brought a feminine glow to the otherwise dark, masculine surroundings. The tall oak dresser and navy-blue bedspread would never be the same.

She sniffed again. "You can turn around now."

Her fuzzy pink robe made him smile. He could almost imagine her wearing a pair of big, fluffy slippers to match. The forlorn expression on her face was hard to swallow, though. He knew Tequila was responsible for her distress. Of course, if Tequila was at fault, then so was he. That knowledge was even harder to swallow.

She hugged herself as if to ward off snake-induced goose bumps. "Will you come in the bathroom with me and stand guard? I have to rinse my hair."

"Me? Stand guard?" *The guy lusting after you?*

She gave a tight little nod. "I can't go back in there by myself. What if the snake is hiding? She might attack me."

Tequila wouldn't attack a mouse, he thought. Okay, a mouse, but not a woman. 'Course, she might be hiding in the drywall somewhere, it was kind of a game he and the snake played. Reptile hide 'n' seek. "Are you *that* scared?"

She nodded again. "Please, Sky."

His pleaded name on her lips was all the encouragement he needed. Fear never sounded sweeter. He wanted to scoop her up in his arms, imaginary bunny slippers and all. "Okay."

Windy tightened her robe. "First I'll have to get dressed."

He cocked his head. "Huh?"

She squinted through red-rimmed eyes, sounding quite prim and proper. "I'm going to wear my swimsuit in the shower."

Unable to control himself, Sky erupted into a fit of boisterous chuckles. Adorable and naive didn't begin to describe her. He didn't normally keep company with innocent little blondes wrapped in cotton-candy robes. "You're somethin' else, Pretty Windy."

Rather than share his mirth, she clenched her teeth. "Don't you dare laugh at me. This is all your fault. You and that snake."

Sky sobered, even though he still felt like grinning. She had no idea how sweet she was. The girlish burst of temper made her look like a hissing kitten trapped in a giant robe, claws bared, matted fur drenched with shampoo. "Sorry. I have sort of a warped sense of humor. I usually laugh at all the wrong times."

She snorted in indignation. "A snake in the shower isn't funny."

"Not to you maybe, but I bet your grandchildren will hoot and holler over it."

Slowly a tiny smile worked its way across Windy's lips. "I suppose you're right about that." Quickly the smile faded. "But you have no idea how much I hate snakes. I've heard stories on the news about pythons, about how they—"

"Tequila's a boa," he interrupted, thinking both pythons and boas made fine companions. "And I swear she won't hurt you. She likes people."

Windy didn't seem convinced. "Will you wait outside my bedroom door while I put my bathing suit on?" She nibbled her lower lip and cast him a nervous glance. "Just in case."

In case what? The snake attacked her? Windy darted into her room, and Sky crossed his arms and leaned against the door. Tequila was harmless. He was the one capable of an attack. After nearly a year of celibacy, the warrior blood was boiling, running through his veins in hot, hungry surges.

About three minutes later she opened the door.

"I'm ready." Pink robe in place, she strode past him.

He followed closely behind.

Too closely. When Windy hesitated at the bathroom door, her abrupt halt caught him off guard. Like an oversize oaf, he bumped right into her.

She gasped and he brought his hands forward, fisting her robe to steady her. Damn. He almost had Pretty Windy in his arms again. Almost. Just ease closer, press your face against the bubbles on her neck, inhale her skin.

Instead he swallowed and released her robe. "I didn't hurt you, did I, honey?"

"Huh? Oh, no, I'm fine." Apparently more concerned

about Tequila's whereabouts than his proximity, she poked her head in the bathroom door. "Will you go in ahead of me?"

"Sure." When he brushed by, Windy reached for his hand.

Sky's breath caught reflexively in his throat. Her feathery touch sent him straight into hormone overdrive. Linking his fingers through hers, he walked slowly through the bathroom, heightening the pleasure, if only for a brief, forbidden moment.

Still holding hands, they neared the bathtub. After making a thorough examination of the surroundings, Windy tugged her hand away. "Go wait over by the sink. And turn around."

Turn around? Jeez, she wore a bathing suit under that robe. After dragging him out of bed and teasing him with that towel display earlier, the least she could do was give him a quick thrill. "Do you keep your robe on when you go to the beach?"

"Dang it, Sky, just turn around."

He almost laughed. The hissing kitten had returned, too tiny to look tough, too sweet to sound menacing. He imagined *dang* was as far as she went.

"Skyler!"

He bit back another grin. Apparently she meant business with the use of his formal name. "You sure are—"

"I mean it, Sky."

A cute little filly. "Okay...okay."

He moved over to the sink, rolled his eyes and turned away. When he heard the spray of water, he wrestled with his conscience. Should he sneak a peek or just imagine what she looked like through the bubbled shower enclosure? Edith Burke's hanky-panky speech sounded in his mind. If that sweet old lady knew what he was up to, she'd skin him alive.

Oh, what the hell. He flashed a wicked grin and turned around.

Windy's robe lay in a heap on the floor. He shook his head. The pile of worn-out terry cloth actually ignited his pulse. Stop now, he told himself, before it's too late.

Naw, he deserved a peek. Just one.

Making a quick mental note to reward Tequila, he sat on

the edge of the sink, stretched out his long legs and leaned over. There she stood, a slim, shadowy figure behind rippled Plexiglas, arms raised, hands moving through her hair. Female flesh and bits of white fabric.

He tilted his head, expanding his view. A tantalizing aroma wafted through the gathering steam, filling his nostrils with a treat: a woman's sweet perfume, vanilla-scented soap. Her damp skin would feel soft, like flower petals after a summer rain, moist and smooth, blooming with color—inviting his caress, his kiss.

It was all in his mind's eye. The two of them together under the warm spray of water, her soapy hands sliding across his chest, his eager hands peeling off her bikini. Mouths tasting, bodies aching. Damn. Sky shifted his hips. The shower steam was rising and so was he.

When Windy opened the enclosure door, he sat staring in her direction. Glassy-eyed, he knew his sinful expression combined hunger and guilt. Feeling like a sneaky child who got caught with his hand in the cookie jar, he grinned—a sheepish don't-punish-me grin.

She reached for her robe, and Sky wondered what to do now. Pretty Windy had him behaving like a randy teenager who didn't have an ounce of control over his raging hormones. And she looked good enough to eat: eyes wide, damp cheeks flushed, wild hair wet and tangled.

Time to hightail it out of here, he thought, planting his feet firmly on the floor. "I'm going to go look for Tequila," he said, racing out the door as if the devil himself were on his heels.

Sky had spent half the day and part of the evening searching for the snake. It was his own fault Tequila was so clever at hiding. Since he had encouraged her throughout the years to play the silly game, she would find a hiding place, poke her head out, then sneak into another spot while his back was turned. He usually tired of the game before she would, so he would abandon the search in favor of a sugary snack and an old-fashioned shoot-'em-up Western. Eventually Tequila would surface, climb onto his lap and fall asleep.

Of course, that had changed, thanks to Windy. Once again, Sky found himself in a bar when he'd rather be lounging in front of the TV. Staying home with her unnerved him. Celibacy was downright self-torture now. A good stiff drink seemed to be the only cure. Well, not the only cure, but Windy might not like the alternative.

This time he avoided the local bar with the nosy cocktail waitress. Today he had headed for a small town in the high desert. To a ratty little dive where people minded their own business. No happy hour. No chic L.A. women. No trendy haircuts. Just a broken-down bar stool, a shot of whiskey and peace of mind.

"Just sit yer butt down and shut up."

Sky knew better than to turn around, but he did it, anyway. The sharp words belonged to a big, crude man, shoving a skittish little redhead through the front door. The man nodded to the bartender, gripped the redhead's arm and seated himself at a table directly behind Sky.

"Bring us a couple of beers," he called out.

"Sure thing, Hank." The bartender waved the rag in his hand.

The woman's timid voice protested softly. "I don't want a beer, Hank. I just want to go home."

"I'm goin' outside for a minute," Hank said, pushing his chair away. "And I don't want to hear you whinin' when I come back. Jimmy's meeting us here for a drink. I'd like to enjoy an evening with my brother for once."

Sky watched the man saunter off, wide shoulders and an even wider girth protruding over grubby, ill-fitting jeans. Hell, damn and hell again. He cursed what he was about to do.

"Are you all right?" He stood at the redhead's table, tapping a pack of cigarettes on his wrist, an old habit he hadn't quite abandoned.

She lifted her chin—empty eyes, pale skin and wiry hair sticking out from the back of a chipped metal clip. She appeared too old to be a runaway, he thought, and too young to look so haggard. As he toyed with the cigarette pack, her eyes grew hungry.

"You want one?"

She nodded and he sat down to light it for her.

"You better go before Hank comes back." She closed her eyes and inhaled, as if savoring something vital. "He has a bad temper."

"Yeah, I kind of figured that," Sky said as the bartender slid Hank's beers onto the table. "What's your name?"

She took another nervous drag. "Lucy."

"How old are you, Lucy?"

"Twenty-three."

Damn. "Hank your boyfriend?"

"Husband," she answered, keeping a close eye on the front door. "We got two kids."

"He do that to you?" Sky reached up to touch the faded bruise on her left cheek.

She looked away. "Why are you talking to me?"

He dropped his hand. Good question. She was twenty-three years old with two kids and an abusive husband. How was he supposed to help? "I thought Hank looked like he needed to pick on someone his own size," he answered, fingering a cigarette. "I don't know much about these things, but I've heard there's places to get help. Women's shelters. I'm sure the police could—"

Lucy interrupted, flicking ashes carelessly. "What are you? A Good Samaritan?"

"No." Sky smiled wryly. "I been called lots of things but Good Sam ain't one of them."

Lucy almost smiled. "You better go, Sam."

He dropped a couple cigarettes on the table. "Nice talking to you, Lucy."

When Sky turned around, he stood eye to eye with Hank. "What were you doin' sitting with my wife, Injun?"

Injun? "Just offering the lady a smoke." Sky noticed there were two Hanks now. Two big, ugly Hanks.

"Stay away from my brother's wife, half-breed," the second Hank said. "We don't like yer kind around here."

Must be Jimmy. Charming family. "Don't know if you boys have heard, but my kind are called Native Americans now." And mixed bloods in the Creek Nation were revered, but he decided to keep that information to himself. One or two of his mixed-blood ancestors may have been chiefs. Now wouldn't that gall Jimmy to think Sky could have descended from Creek royalty?

Hank reached for the cigarettes on the table. Shoving them against Sky's chest, he flashed a cocky grin to his brother. "Take your smokes and go, blue eyes."

Sky's jaw twitched as Hank crumbled the cigarettes against his chest. What he wouldn't give to ram his fist down this man's throat. But his days of brawling in bars were over. "I'll just go finish my drink."

"You do that." Jimmy gave him a little shove. Instinctively Sky's fists clenched.

Don't do it, he told himself. A couple of rednecks aren't worth a night in jail. What possessed him to stop at this hole-in-the-wall, anyway? How many times had he been in similar situations? Honky-tonk bars in the middle of nowhere. Truckers, bikers, rednecks, other cowboys. He'd brawled with them all. The smart thing to do—get out and don't look back. "Like I said, I'll go finish my drink."

Hank and Jimmy sat their wide behinds down, and Sky could hear Hank cussing at Lucy. Damn, he had only made things worse for her.

And then he spent the next two hours thinking about another woman—a pretty little blonde. Why did he find Windy so appealing? Was it her innocence? Her gentle nature? When she'd caught him ogling her through the shower door, he'd embarrassed them both, yet she hadn't snapped at him. And the fact that she didn't kind of warmed his innards.

Sky fingered the cigarette pack. Forget about her. You gave up women months ago. And for good reason. The more he remembered about his past, the more he realized his inability to love, to participate in a healthy relationship. And substituting sex for love was one of those weird Freudian things he wanted no conscious part of.

What decent woman would want him, anyway? Especially a woman dedicating her life to children. What he'd done made him a dishonorable man, a first-class, A1 bastard. The kind of guy who didn't have the right to look at a woman like Windy, let alone fantasize about her.

Sky pushed his hair out of his eyes. He knew Windy found him attractive. He'd caught her admiring glances, her lowered lashes and soft smile. Spoiling that attraction would be easy, though. All he'd have to do was tell her that he'd been a teenage father who had abandoned his son, a guy too selfish to accept his parental responsibilities, too screwed up to know how to love someone else.

He tapped on his empty shot glass. He wanted to find his kid and set things right. But how could he? He had yet to remember the boy's name, who the child's mother was, or exactly what had happened.

The *child*. Hell, by now his son would be about seventeen—practically a man. Sky closed his eyes. Hopefully a better one than himself.

Rough, masculine voices grabbed his attention, interrupting his thoughts. He opened his eyes and frowned. The commotion: Hank and Jimmy at the door, drunk as skunks with Lucy wrestling Hank for the keys to his car.

"Hank, honey, let me drive." A victim's words, softly spoken.

Sky squeezed his eyes shut again, but the coward's way out didn't help. He could smell Lucy's fear. Frail little Lucy, afraid to run. Afraid not to. He gripped his chair as if to keep himself in it. Someone else's troubles were none of his business. He had plenty of his own.

He motioned to the bartender. "Isn't it your responsibility to keep people from driving drunk?"

The bartender, fortyish, large arms inked with tattoos a man might receive from another inmate, grunted like an angry bear. "Hank ain't that drunk."

No, not that drunk. Sky watched Hank and Jimmy stumble out the door, Lucy fretting nervously behind them.

Damn. "Give me another one." He slid the shot glass toward the tattooed bear. If he was going to brawl with a couple of redneck brothers then another belt of whiskey was definitely in order.

The gold liquid burned his throat. This is my last night in a bar, he told himself. Pretty roommate or not. Sky had the sinking feeling he was about to get his butt kicked. Hank and Jimmy might be drunk, but there were still two of them.

Well, hell. He headed for the door. If getting roughed up a little meant giving Lucy the chance to snag those car keys, then it would be well worth it.

The cheery ladybugs on the kitchen border did nothing to improve Windy's mood. She poured herself a glass of filtered tap water, placed it on the oak tabletop, then peered into the living room, checking on the snake's whereabouts for the hundredth time. It appeared to be sleeping, resting lazily in its glass domain. Even though she told herself being fearful wasted positive energy, and reptiles were one of God's creations, its slimy presence still gave her the creeps. At least it hadn't escaped again. As long as that beast remained caged, she could learn to deal with it.

Sky, on the other hand, was another matter. He had been gone all night, and that bothered Windy. She had been thinking far too much about her roommate, feeling much too attracted to him.

Where would a man go all night? She headed for the refrigerator and pulled the door open. The disturbing answer was as plain as the nose on her face. To a woman's house, of course. He had spent the night with a woman. Another woman.

My God. She was actually jealous. Jealous of Sky smiling at another woman, touching another woman, kissing another woman. She slipped a slice of wheat bread into the toaster and admonished herself. Sky had the right to a personal life, and a man who looked like him probably had plenty of lovers. Dang it. Why should she care? She barely knew him.

Windy sat at the kitchen table and nibbled her dry toast. The problem, she decided, was Sky's mysterious background. Once she talked to Edith, and Sky's secrets were disclosed, maybe she would quit obsessing about him. She couldn't help but recall that shower and every erotic, awkward detail. Every tingling sensation. She had practically melted on the spot while his fevered gaze slid sensuously over her flesh, his boyish smile rife with mischief. No point in denying the primal urges that had loomed in the steam-filled air.

Windy frowned. Primal urges she had never experienced before. Textbook knowledge aside, sexual promiscuity remained an enigma in her mind. She couldn't imagine intimacy without love, yet here she was, falling in lust with a stranger—a gorgeous, troubled stranger. A summer fling was out of the question, though. She had saved herself for a lifetime of love and commitment, not a season of dusty boots, faded jeans and the most incredible blue eyes imaginable.

The sound of the front door opening jolted Windy's heart. Sky was home, his footsteps unmistakable. Should she turn around? Pretend she wasn't thinking about him? Toss her head carelessly and say hello? Force a casual smile? Avoid his eyes?

Oh, yes, she should definitely avoid those blue eyes.

"Hey, Pretty Windy," his husky voice caressed her.

Take a deep breath. Turn around and face him.

"Oh, my God, Sky, what happened to you?"

There he stood: Western shirt, bloodstained and torn; jeans filthy; turned-up boots dustier than usual. A blackened eye. Dirt and dried blood caked in the corners of slightly swollen lips.

"Had a little accident."

Windy's pulse raced. "A car accident?"

His good eye twitched. "Naw, my face had an accident with someone's fist."

She shook her head. Someone's fist? He'd been in a fight? All at once she felt maternal, disgusted and confused. She wanted to reprimand him, yet hold him. Tell him off soundly, yet wipe the blood from his chin and ease the swelling.

"Let me guess. You were drinking last night and got into a brawl. Oh, and there was a woman involved."

"Sorta…well, yeah." He frowned. "I wasn't drunk, though. And there were two of them."

"Two women? You had a fight over two women."

"No." His frown deepened, creasing the space between his eyebrows. "I had a fight with two men. There was only one woman. She was married to one of the men. Her husband was a jerk."

Windy didn't know what to say or what to do. He looked miserable, yet he had brought it upon himself. She didn't believe in violence of any kind. "You fought with this lady's husband because he was jerk?"

"Yeah. Sorta, I guess."

She sighed, the teacher in her taking over. On occasion the boys in her class pushed and shoved. She knew how to talk them out of a skirmish, and when it was too late, bandage a scraped knee and hug their hurt away. She studied Sky. Did he need someone to hug the hurt away?

"Why don't you sit down and tell me what happened while I get you cleaned up."

He shifted his feet as though debating her offer, debating whether or not to let her touch him. She couldn't help but smile. Some of her tough-guy students did that, too. They held their little faces high and bit back their tears.

"I'll be gentle. I promise."

His bloodied lips broke into a grin, warming her from head to toe. He inched forward, his hair falling across his black eye. "Okay, Nurse Windy, you're on."

Oh, no, she thought. I'm in trouble. Even bruised and battered, her mysterious roommate had an engaging smile—a smile guarding the man within. The man she longed to know.

Three

It hurt like hell to grin, but Sky couldn't help himself. No woman had ever made a sweeter offer. She said something about getting the first-aid kit and he watched her walk down the hall. She looked fresh: purple flowers sprinkled across her spring-green dress; legs bare; painted toenails slung into leather sandals. He hoped she had a first-aid kit. He knew he didn't.

Windy returned and placed a stack of towels, several wash-cloths and a first-aid kit on the oak tabletop. The red cross on the plastic container and the clean white cloths seemed official. Sky slid his long body into a chair and smiled again.

"Would you stop grinning." She touched the corner of his mouth with a damp cloth. "You're making your lips bleed."

He closed his eyes and winced like a child being scrubbed clean by his mother. And then he fidgeted, feeling like a little boy as she ran her hands through the front of his hair, moving it away from his face. He couldn't remember anyone ever fussing over him—babying or mothering him. He decided he liked the attention, maybe always longed for it, even though, like now, he probably didn't deserve it.

"I'm not hurting you, am I?" she asked.

God, no. "The hair part feels good."

Her hand stilled. "You have beautiful hair."

When he opened his eyes, the swollen one fluttered, causing him to squint. Her compliment embarrassed him a little, so he chose to change the subject by skipping the "thank you" part. "The fight was my fault, I guess. But I'm not sorry about it. That guy at the bar, he was treatin' his wife bad, so I called him on it. She was a little bit of a thing. Like you, Pretty Windy. Just a slip of a girl."

"Oh."

Sky figured she didn't know what else to say. He'd made it sound as though it had been *her* honor he'd defended. She moved the damp cloth down his neck, and he unbuttoned his torn shirt. Suddenly, being this close to her didn't seem like such a good idea.

"Oh, Sky," Windy's voice reached out compassionately. "What did they do to you?" His unbuttoned shirt exposed a colorful patch of bruising on his chest and stomach.

Feeling a little foolish, he shrugged. "Got kicked a few times." Ugly Hank had big feet and big, steel-toed boots. "Nothing's broken. And I got in a few good kicks of my own. I got one of them in the...ah—" Sky remembered Jimmy, hunched over, his face twisted in pain. "Well, I got him good."

Windy stared at his marred flesh, then raised her eyes to his grinning face. "This isn't funny. You look awful."

"I've been hurt worse. This ain't nothin'." He realized how ridiculously macho he sounded and how poor his grammar was. Ladylike women put him on guard, making him feel inadequate in ways he couldn't begin to describe. Flashing a disarming grin was his only defense, that or flirting.

Windy doused a cotton ball with a strong antiseptic. Gently dabbing it at his chest, she cleaned the bloodied scrapes surrounding the bruises. "Do you get into a lot of fights?"

"Used to," he responded. "It's the cowboy way, I suppose."

Her caramel-colored eyes locked onto his. "What does that mean exactly?"

Surviving the loneliness, he wanted to say. Having to prove you're a man. "It's just a life-style."

She doused another cotton ball. "Sounds dangerous."

He laughed, his lip splitting a little as he did. It was, he supposed. Stupid and dangerous. "Charlie never went out for that sort of thing, though. Used to give me hell about it." But then, his boss had a wife and daughter. He didn't understand what it felt like to be completely alone. "Charlie's a responsible cowboy."

She smiled. "I have a feeling I'd like Charlie. How long have you worked for him?"

"Seems like forever." Sky's gaze followed Windy's hands. They were tending his stomach now. There wasn't much to doctor, just a few minor scrapes. The bruises would heal on their own. "Charlie's been good to me." But Sky wasn't always loyal to Charlie. He'd pop in and out of the other cowboy's life, work for him sporadically. Sky couldn't take the show-biz thing year round so he'd find ranch work in between. Maybe it wasn't just the show-biz aspect, he thought. Maybe he feared the affection he felt for Charlie's family, the wondering about his own.

Windy studied him as though trying to read his mind. Her being a psychology student made him uneasy. He didn't like being analyzed, especially by a decent woman. If she looked deep enough, she wouldn't like what she saw.

"Where are you from originally?" she asked.

He shrugged evasively. "Nowhere. Everywhere. I get restless, move a lot. I enjoy a change of scenery." How could he tell her he didn't know where he was born, or who his people were? Or that he had recurring nightmares about a tiny gray-eyed boy and a hawk? Sky blew an exhausted breath. Dreams of hawks, dreams of his son. Nothing in his head made any sense. Was the hawk his son's protector? Was it angry at Sky for what he'd done to the boy? Or was the hawk appearing in his dreams strictly as a messenger, sending messages he didn't understand? He knew animal medicine carried great power—power one shouldn't misinterpret.

Windy studied Sky's frown. What was he thinking? Oh, for Pete's sake, he was probably disturbed by her question. The man had amnesia. He probably didn't remember where he was from. Edith had said he knew very little about himself.

Windy sighed and tossed the soiled cotton balls into a plastic bag. She wished he would confide in her. He needed to trust someone. Why not a woman exploring the human psyche?

"You done?" Sky asked. "I got a few scrapes on my back. Will you take a look at them?"

She nodded. It appeared he found comfort in her medical ministrations. "You'll have to take your shirt off."

"No problem." He removed the torn garment hastily, as if resisting the urge to shred it. There wasn't much left of it, Windy noted. It had been a nice shirt, detailed with silver piping and nickel buttons. She wasn't surprised that he'd destroyed something of quality. He probably did that often. He didn't appear to value material items.

"The cuts are down here." He touched his lower back. "It might be hard for you to reach them if I'm sittin' down. Should I stand up, maybe?"

Windy took a deep breath, his big, bronzed chest suddenly making her ill at ease. "Sure."

He stood, turned his back, then jolted forward. "Damn." He winced, clutching his midsection.

There were a few cuts low on his back, just as he'd said, but she decided they weren't the problem. The bruises on his stomach had to hurt. She couldn't imagine being kicked there.

She placed her hands on his shoulders. "Are you all right?"

"Yeah. I'll be fine. I just got stiff sitting for so long, I guess."

"Oh, I'm sorry." Offering comfort, she allowed her hands

to express her concern. For an instant she kneaded his shoulders, then made consoling strokes through his hair.

Seeping through the protective shell of Sky's rough-and-tumble ego was a thin veil of vulnerability. It circled around Windy like the sweetened smoke of incense, begging for more of her compassion, her touch.

He needed her.

And she needed him. Needed to explore the breadth of his shoulders, the silky hair falling down his back. Windy combed through the thickness, capturing the midnight strands in between her fingers.

She felt him shudder, saw the muscles ripple down his back, listened to his pleasured sigh. Although she touched him tentatively, Sky responded as though he wanted to fall into her arms. Hold her close. Kiss her.

But when he turned abruptly to face her, a thick silence fell between them.

For several uncomfortable moments they stared at each other, aware of the heat passing between them. They stood paralyzed, suspended in time, her fingers frozen in his hair, his eyes as silent as a vast summer sky. She inhaled his scent: blood, sweat and traces of peppermint candy. The unusual combination sent a tingle down her spine.

Windy moved her throat just enough to swallow. She had no business encouraging him, not in a romantic way. He might want more than she was willing to give. Drop your hand. Step back.

Oh, my God. Mortified, she glanced away. Somehow her ring had become caught in his hair, twisted in the heavy black mass.

Whispering an apology, she tugged gently in an effort to release her hand, trying for a noncommittal focus. In spite of herself, her gaze met his, spicing her blood until it seared through her veins. Immediately her knees weakened. If her legs buckled, she would either pull Sky to the ground with her or tear out a handful of his hair before collapsing.

Still struggling to gain control, Windy gauged Sky's reaction. He was going to say something. Do something. Make a joke. Pretend this was amusing. With that warped sense of humor, he probably thought this was amusing.

On cue, his slightly damaged lips curved into a big, lopsided smile.

Windy's breath expanded. "I suppose we do look rather silly," she said, her legs regaining their consistency. "But if you laugh—"

Her warning came too late; he was already laughing.

"Sky, this is not funny. My ring is stuck in your hair. And you're splitting your lip again."

He made a face at her. A hideous face, which she thought effective with the addition of his black eye. Giggling seemed her only option. She had never met anyone quite like him. "You're a strange man." She felt him pulling at her hand. "What are you doing?"

"Getting your hand out of my hair."

She stepped back and wiggled her finger, displaying Sky's handiwork. Attached to the ruby ring were several long strands of black hair. They exchanged a quick burst of laughter.

He lifted an eyebrow. "So I'm strange, huh?"

Strange. Gorgeous. Mysterious. She could hardly wait to talk to Edith about him. Windy glanced at the microwave clock. In two hours she would be sipping tea at Edith's house. "You make some weird faces."

He shrugged and spied the coffeepot. "Is that fresh?"

"I made it about an hour ago."

"Good enough." He strolled over to the counter, poured a cup, then added an enormous amount of sugar.

She watched in fascination. Odd. He struck her as the kind of bar-brawling cowboy who would prefer his coffee strong and bitter.

He tasted the dark brew, winced and reached for the sugar bowl once again. She tidied the mess on the table and tried not to laugh. "Why don't you have a little coffee with your sugar, Sky?"

He flashed his signature smile. "I have a sweet tooth."

Her heart warmed and fluttered. How could a man be virile and boyish at the same time? Rough yet gentle? Strong yet vulnerable?

Windy sat at the table and pushed a loose strand of hair away from her face. Her lack of experience was showing. She understood children, not men. At twenty-six, she'd been dating less than ten years, but never serious dates, or long-term boyfriends. Although plenty of men found her attractive, she'd never lost her heart, made earth-shattering love or even cuddled in masculine arms all night. Call her old-fashioned, but she didn't mind waiting for the real thing.

What would it be like to sleep next to Sky? she wondered. To curl up beside that long, copper body? Feel those rippling muscles? Old-fashioned or not, a girl had the right to dream, didn't she?

Sky clanked a spoon against his cup. Windy looked up with a start to find him watching her, a knowing look in his eye. Uncomfortable, she fussed with her hair again—hair that curled haphazardly no matter what the style or length. She pushed an annoying ringlet away, but it sprang back, slapping her cheek. This time an exasperated huff blew it behind her shoulder. A moment later it returned.

Sky's dimples surfaced. "You have bedroom hair."

"Excuse me?"

He came forward, coffee cup in hand. "Your hair looks as if you just tumbled out of bed." He wiggled his eyebrows. "Nothing's sexier than a thoroughly loved woman with tangled hair."

Windy tried not to blush. For Pete's sake. What a thing for him to say, especially after she'd been fantasizing about sleeping in his arms. "My hair always looks like this." And she'd never been thoroughly loved.

He leaned on the table, his husky voice low and intimate. "Say, Pretty Windy with the bedroom hair, are you hungry?"

Her pulse raced. "Hungry?"

He chuckled. "Yeah. For food. You know, breakfast."

Windy regained her composure. Her flirtatious new roommate had a dastardly sense of humor. Hungry indeed. He knew darn well the way he'd made it sound. "I would imagine you're ready to eat."

"Hell, yes. I got the tar beat out of me last night, slept in my truck, then brushed my teeth in a service station rest room. I'm downright starving."

She couldn't imagine living such an irresponsible life-style. "I can fix you something. I always keep a well-stocked fridge."

He smiled. "Sure, okay. It would save me the trouble of going back out again."

Windy's mood brightened. There were advantages to having a male roommate. Security, safety. Someone to haul the trash cans out to the curb, someone to fix the plumbing, someone to cook for. She wasn't used to having a man around. Sky would be the first man with whom she had shared a home. Her father had died when she was still small, and her mother never remarried.

"What would you like to eat?" she asked.

He shrugged. "Anything. A bowl of oatmeal, frozen waffles. Don't go to any trouble on my account."

"It's no trouble. I like to cook. I even enjoy going to the market."

He placed his empty coffee cup in the sink. "Really? Well, maybe you could shop for me, too. I could give you some money and you could add my stuff to yours. Mostly I just keep snacks around. Candy, chips, stuff like that."

Windy smiled. So the big strong cowboy liked junk food. "No problem."

Sky leaned against the counter as she rummaged through the refrigerator. "You're different from most California girls."

She looked up. "I am? How so?"

He cocked his head. "Well, you're blond and all that, but you're domestic."

She wasn't quite certain how to take the unusual comment. "I guess you don't know many women who like to cook."

"Not ones as pretty as you." He closed the first-aid kit. "Does this go in the bathroom?"

She nodded. He had a way of saying whatever came to mind. And although his compliments weren't offhanded, they weren't polished, either. Of course, neither was he.

Sky gathered the soiled cloths and stacked them on top of the first-aid kit. "I'm gonna take a shower. I won't be long."

"Okay."

Enjoying her task, Windy hummed as she cracked eggs into a bowl and added a dash of milk. Next she diced onions and mushrooms, then scooped them into a separate bowl. Before starting the pancake batter, she opened the freezer. Some pre-seasoned hash browns should please Sky as well as a tall glass of orange juice. A simple fruit salad would follow: apples, grapes, bananas, a little whipped cream, tiny marshmallows.

She supposed her domestic qualities weren't hard to miss. Although she intended to have a successful career, she also wanted a husband and a house full of children. And she didn't mind admitting it one bit. Too many people didn't appreciate family values. In her opinion being a parent was the most important job in the world.

And now Sky's virile presence and charming smile made her long even more for what she didn't have. A husband. A family. Strange that a man like him could encourage that yearning. Handsome, blue-eyed Sky. The reckless drifter. The rebellious cowboy. Engaging, but not husband material.

When Sky returned, breakfast waited on the table. He stood stiffly at first, staring at the food. Windy wondered if the loner in him wanted to run from the domestic welcome. Luckily the other side of him, the bright-eyed boy, smiled and pulled up a chair. "This looks good."

Windy poured juice in their glasses, then joined him at the table. She noticed he'd changed into loose-fitting sweatpants. His wet hair looked even longer and his scent suggested a deodorized bar of soap, fresh yet masculine. His bare chest glistened, even through the bruises. Strange, but the purplish discoloration didn't seem to detract from his charm. They only reminded her of his dangerous, if not heroic, nature.

"You're not eating much," he remarked.

She glanced down at the small portions on her plate. "I had some toast earlier."

Sky attacked his food with gusto, pouring a glob of ketchup over his hash browns. Apparently she had done well, choosing foods he liked. He drenched the pancakes in syrup and moaned when he tasted the omelet. "Do you bake? Cookies, pies. Stuff like that?"

She did for her students on occasion. A vegetarian who counted her caloric intake, Windy rarely indulged in sinful desserts. At the moment Sky reminded her of one of those treats. Mouthwatering and forbidden.

"I bake around the holidays. Pies at Thanksgiving. Cookies and brownies at Christmas."

"Edith bakes for me," he said.

"What's your favorite dessert?"

Sky looked up and laughed. "You don't want to know."

Windy tried to guess. "Something with lots of chocolate? Mud pie or double-fudge cake?"

"Nope."

She sent him a smug smile. "I can always ask Edith."

"Honey, this isn't something Edith knows about." His raised eyebrow made him look wicked, especially with the cuts and bruises. "A pretty woman who smells like vanilla ice cream isn't something I could tell the old lady to whip up."

Vanilla ice cream? A pretty woman? Windy narrowed her eyes. "You're teasing me because of my perfume."

"Maybe." He reached for the fruit salad, his lips working into a smile. "Then maybe not."

She decided it was time to stand up to his machismo. "You're a flirt, Sky."

"Yeah." The smile turned crooked. "I guess I am."

She wagged her finger, reprimanding him like the modern schoolmarm she was. "I'm used to men flirting. So quit trying to embarrass me. It won't work."

Amusement slipped into his grin. "So it won't embarrass you if I tell you that you remind me of Lady Godiva?"

Lady Godiva, the woman who supposedly rode naked on horseback? Although her heart had dived for her throat, she managed an unaffected shrug. "No."

"She was the blonde, the one with all the hair who—"

Windy interrupted quickly "I know who she was." For Pete's sake, she didn't need him mentioning the naked part.

Sky finished the last of the fruit salad and reached for his drink. "So, Pretty Windy, do you like to ride?"

"Horses?" Lord, no. She had fallen from one when she was a child. "I think they're beautiful but I don't ride." That sounded better than saying she was too nervous to get back on.

Sky leaned forward. "I could teach you. Trail riding is something everyone should experience. A loyal horse and Mother Earth, there's nothing else like it."

He made it sound romantic. "I don't know. I'm—" She chewed her lip. "I'm—"

"Afraid?" he interjected.

She nodded. Afraid of snakes, afraid of horses. She must have sounded like a basket case—a psychologist who needed her own therapist. "I was bucked off when I was little."

Instead of the teasing retort she expected, his voice softened. "I'd be patient. Charlie has some gentle trail horses. But if you're too afraid to mount up by yourself, you could ride with me. In my culture, horses represent power and wealth. And spiritually a horse could enable a holy man to fly through the air in search of Heaven." His gaze sought hers. "We could take a trip to Heaven."

Windy's pulse hammered. Lord, he was beautiful. Did he know how enticing his offer was? "I need to think about it," she said, telling herself to beware. He would only be in town for three months. A trip to Heaven might leave her yearning for more.

When the conversation lulled, they sat in awkward silence. She toyed with her napkin while he studied the kitchen walls.

Now she understood why he flirted. Acknowledging their attraction was easier that way.

Quickly Windy hopped up and began clearing the table. Sky offered to help. As they busied themselves, her brain went into its rational mode. Flirting, even fantasizing was one thing, but falling prey to his charms was another. She imagined summer flings suited him just fine. They were not for her.

He rinsed the dishes, and she loaded them into the dishwasher, but when he glanced up at the window, a glass slipped from his hand. It shattered into the sink.

Windy jumped back, recalling the day her home had been vandalized—the broken china, smashed stereo and cracked television screen. For a brief moment, the fear and nausea returned.

She took a deep, cleansing breath. This was just an accident, that was...

She looked over at Sky. He stood gazing out the window, his hands trembling.

"Are you all right?" she asked, her own discomfort immediately forgotten.

"Huh?" He turned toward her, his eyes glazed, his voice mechanical. "There was a hawk outside the window."

A hawk? Why would the sight of a bird make him tremble to the point of dropping a glass? "Are you sure you're okay?"

"Yeah. It just seemed weird that it came so close to the house. Startled me, that's all."

But why? "Are hawks dangerous?"

"No." He smiled a bit nervously. "Not unless you're a rodent."

She peered out the tiny kitchen window yet saw nothing but the neighbor's fence and the trees beyond it. "Do you think it was searching for food?"

"Maybe."

He raked his hands through his damp hair, and she noticed they appeared steadier. Maybe he had the right to be jumpy. He had, after all, been in a fight the night before. Then again, a hawk? Maybe she should question Edith about it. Sky certainly wasn't an easy man to understand.

"I'm sorry I broke your glass," he said.

Windy touched his shoulder. "Don't worry about it. I'm going shopping today, anyway. It's about time to replace all those other broken dishes. I borrowed the ones we just used."

Sky removed the shattered glass from the sink, carefully lifting the larger pieces first. "Do you need some money? I'd be glad to help out."

"You don't have to do that. I can charge what I need." She glanced at the red digits on the microwave clock. "I hope you don't mind, but I should probably get going."

She had a meeting with Edith—a meeting she didn't intend to miss.

Four

Edith Burke's living room made Windy feel at home, in an old-fashioned kind of way. The dated furnishings could be called Early-American-Grandmother style: polished maple tables, a cuckoo clock that chimed every hour, an avocado-and-gold sofa, crocheted doilies. Even the outside of the wooden structure shouted Grandma, with its small, manicured lawn and hummingbird feeders. Edith wasn't a grandmother, though. The elderly widow didn't have children of her own.

Windy seated herself in an overstuffed chair and crossed her legs. She watched Edith place a silver tea set on the coffee table and arrange china cups and saucers. The retired teacher often wore an apron and orthopedic shoes, her silver hair professionally coifed. Windy smiled, imagining Edith at the beauty parlor, her thinning hair wrapped in pink curlers.

"Something smells good," Windy said. Edith's home always had a fresh-baked scent, an aroma that made a house feel like a home.

"I fried some round pieces of bread dough, then sprinkled

powdered sugar over them.'' Edith smoothed her apron.
"They're one of Sky's favorite treats. He says they remind
him of Indian fry-bread." She held up a slightly bent finger.
"I'll bring you a platter, and what you don't eat you can take
home."

Windy, anxious to get their conversation underway, poured
the tea while Edith scurried into the kitchen.

"Here you go." The older lady handed her a plate of the
warm pastries. "I suppose they're the European version of fry-
bread. I have no idea what to call them. My Italian grandmother used to make them when I was a child."

Windy didn't know what Indian fry-bread was, but the cir-
cles of fried dough on the platter looked like thick, puffy
clouds. She envisioned Sky devouring each one and licking
the powdered sugar from his fingers.

She placed a napkin on her lap and nibbled the unusual
pastry. "This is wonderful. Perfect with tea." And probably
packed with calories.

Edith cocked her head in a birdlike pose. "A little treat now
and again won't hurt you."

Windy grinned. "You always could read my mind."

"True." The widow added lemon to her tea, sat on the sofa
and sipped carefully. "And what a bright mind it is."

"Thanks." Lately her mind had been tuned to one channel.
One tall, blue-eyed channel, which made small talk useless at
this point. "Tell me about Sky's accident, Edith. Everything
you can remember."

"Oh, my." The other woman placed a liver-spotted hand
against her bosom. "Where do I start?" She gazed up at the
ceiling as though collecting her thoughts. "It all happened so
fast. One minute I was pushing the traffic-light button, waiting
to cross the street, the next I heard the squeal of tires."

Windy knew the accident had happened near the Equestrian
Center, which accounted for Sky's presence there. He must
have been working in the area.

Edith continued in a quiet voice. "I would have been hit if
it hadn't been for Sky. He ran up shouting, then pushed me

out of the way. That car missed me by inches. Sky wasn't so lucky.''

"How badly was he hurt?"

"He was in a coma for weeks. The doctors weren't sure if he would pull through. Of course, he did. That boy is a fighter."

"Yes, he is." In more ways than one, Windy thought, picturing Sky's recent black eye. "So when he came out of the coma, he had amnesia?"

Edith nodded. "He suffered a trauma, but no brain damage. Which means it's possible his memory may return someday."

"Just how much does he remember?"

"Not much. When he first came to, he knew his first name was Skyler and that he worked for a man named Charlie."

"Wasn't Charlie able to help? Sky must have talked about himself before the accident."

"Unfortunately Charlie didn't have much to offer. At that time Sky had only worked for him for a few weeks. And since cowboys tend to drift quite a bit, Charlie didn't ask Sky a lot of personal questions. They talked horses mostly."

"What about the police? I mean, here's this man who doesn't know who he is or where he came from. Couldn't they trace Sky's background from his driver's license or Social Security card? Or run a credit check on him for a previous address? Find his family somehow?"

"This is where it gets complicated." She smoothed the starched blue apron in a gesture that seemed like habit, then frowned a little at her next words. "The police said the identification Sky had on him was false."

False? Windy's heart slammed against her ribs. "You mean he had a fake ID? Why?"

"According to the police, there could have been a number of reasons."

"Like what?"

"Criminal activity for one—"

Windy's jaw dropped as her pulse picked up speed. "Oh, my God. You mean—"

"Calm down, dear." Although the older woman still frowned, she interrupted in a steady voice, a voice that didn't react to panic. "Sky's not a hoodlum. The police fingerprinted him and didn't come up with anything."

The tension in Windy's stomach refused to relax, turning the sweet herbal tea sour. She had a man living in her house who had purposely concealed his identity. "Why would someone use a fake ID if they didn't have something to hide?"

"You have to remember this was sixteen years ago, which means Sky may have been a minor. Plenty of minors sneak into bars with those fake IDs," Edith responded, her eyes dark beneath pale gray brows. "And there's also the possibility he may have been a runaway. That, too, would explain the false ID."

A runaway. The thought made Windy sad. The streets were mean to minors, and she doubted Sky would have fared any better than today's troubled youth. "What did the police think?"

"They believed that he'd used the ID for both purposes. That he was a runaway who needed a dummy ID and decided to make himself twenty-one in the process."

"Does that mean Skyler Reed isn't even his real name?"

"It's hard to say." Emotion overtook the other woman, causing her steady, teacher's voice to quaver. "Can you imagine how I felt? Here was this brave young man who had risked his life to save mine. And except for Charlie, whom he had only known for two weeks, he was all alone."

How awful, Windy thought, that no one was searching for him, missing him. "What was Sky like then?"

"He had a rebellious sort of charm. You know, street smart. I could see where he had fooled people with that ID." Edith managed a fond smile. "Oh, of course, there was that vulnerable side of him, too. The boy on the verge of manhood."

"How old do you think he was?"

"The police figured him to be about seventeen."

Windy tried to picture Sky as a street-smart youth in torn jeans and worn-soled boots, passing himself off as a man. She imagined him just as tall, yet leaner, less muscular. His hair would have been long then, too, and his eyes gorgeous but guarded. "Did he seem afraid?"

Edith nodded. "Confused and afraid and trying hard not to show it. He's come a long way." She sighed. "But he still has a hard time accepting affection, even though I think he's starving for it."

Windy couldn't quell the maternal fluttering that Edith's statement caused. Sky was a grown man, yet she felt compelled to mother him, hold him close and erase the pain from his past, the possible ugliness. Teenagers don't run away from happy homes. Then again, people often flee from their own deeds. He could have done something that shamed his family, a moral indiscretion.

"Do you think he remembers things that make him uncomfortable? Things he'd prefer not to talk about?" she asked.

"Maybe." Edith refilled her cup and added her usual squeeze of lemon. "I'm aware that he doesn't tell me everything. He's a young man and I'm an old woman—confidentiality isn't in our favor." She tasted the tea. "I adore him, but I'm not naive. I know he's still a bit of a hellion."

"A hellion with a heroic nature," Windy said. "He's wild and reckless, but trustworthy. Of course, you already knew that, or you wouldn't have suggested him for my roommate." Her stomach settling, she reached for her tea. "I can't help but like him."

The older woman leaned forward and patted her hand. "I knew you would."

A warmth spread through Windy. Edith had always treated her like family. "Has Sky ever mentioned hawks to you? He noticed one this morning outside of the kitchen window and seemed unnerved by it."

"Really?" She brought a finger to her mouth and tapped it against her thin, aging lips. "Sky believes in animal totems. I know that ravens represent magic, but I'm not sure what power the hawk possesses. You'd have to ask him."

"I will." Windy intended to pick her new roommate's brain

as thoroughly as he would allow. "I have some shopping to do, but I'll talk to Sky when I get back."

Sky reclined in a leather chair, watching television. When Windy opened the front door, he turned to face her, already missing the solitude. He still wasn't used to having a roommate, especially a shapely blonde.

"What did you do, buy out the whole place?" The woman carried at least four large department-store bags.

"Maybe I did go a little overboard. There's more stuff in the car."

"I'll go," he offered, grabbing the keys from her hand.

Windy protested, making an unsuccessful attempt to retrieve her keys. "I can bring in my own packages. You're injured, you need to sit still."

Sit still? Hell, he'd been sitting still all day. Ignoring Windy's exasperated sigh, Sky dashed out to her Honda—a well-maintained, practical model, he mused. He drove a '59 Chevy pickup he'd restored himself. The turquoise Apache gave him pleasure, even if it still had drum brakes and lacked power steering.

Within minutes he crashed back through the door, dumping bags and boxes onto the sofa.

Windy, he noticed, had slipped into the chair he'd deserted, studying him as though taking inventory of his character. What did she hope to find? Integrity? A sense of honor? Responsibility? If she looked deep enough, she'd be disappointed. He didn't have anything to offer a woman like her.

Sky shifted his stance and focused on her packages. He moved closer to the sofa to inspect one of the boxes. "Did you buy a pair of boots?" he asked, recognizing the manufacturer's name printed on the box.

Windy blinked, and he figured she hadn't found the character traits in him she'd been searching for. He knew she never would.

"You can open it if you'd like to see them," she said.

"All right." He flipped up the box top, then lifted one shiny black boot. "Hey, these are nice. Flashy."

"Thanks."

She smiled appreciatively, and his stomach fluttered. Did she buy them to impress him? Certain they were her first pair of Western boots, he wondered if she was considering his offer to teach her to ride.

"They're lizard," she said. "I'd thought about snakeskin, but—" she glanced at Tequila's cage "—I didn't want to offend anyone."

Sky placed the boot back in the box. Her soft, teasing smile made him want to flirt. Goose bumps had crept up her arm, and he couldn't help but wonder if he or the snake had caused them.

He knew he possessed the power to visibly maul her, so he did it, no matter how wrong. He thought of it as "mind sex," the safest encounter a celibate man could have.

Sky braced his back against the wall and dove into his fantasy—raking his gaze over her slender body. Although Windy wore a fresh, almost wholesome dress, she looked provocative against the black leather. Wild in an innocent way. A full mouth. Tumbling locks.

Windy didn't miss his lewd appraisal. She brought the recliner forward as though suddenly conscious of her bare legs. "I saw Edith earlier," she said in an apparent attempt to redirect his attention.

Sky continued to disrobe her with his eyes, imagining every feminine swell and lethal curve. A strand of her hair had adhered itself to her glossy lips. He envisioned himself licking it away.

She pushed the unruly hair back into place. "Edith told me about the accident and what happened to you."

Damn it. So much for mind sex. He felt as if a bucket of water had dropped from the ceiling, dousing him with ice-cold reality. "You talked to Edith about me?"

She nodded. "You told me to. Remember?"

His own words haunted him like a disloyal ghost. *I'd really prefer you talk to Edith about this.* "So you know I have amnesia?"

She nodded again, but took the conversation in another direction. "I asked her about hawks, too. She told me that you believe in animal totems. What does that mean?"

Damn. Pretty Windy had slipped on her psychologist's coat like a nosy little chameleon. He sensed she'd be drilling him for the rest of the day. "It's a heritage thing. Native Americans believe in wacky stuff."

She scooted to the edge of the chair. "You don't think it's wacky or you wouldn't believe in it."

He gave her credit for gentle persistence. "Animals carry medicine, healing powers. They teach us how to live in harmony with Mother Earth. A person's totem protects them and gives them special gifts."

She appeared intrigued, her caramel eyes alight with curiosity. "How can people tell what animal is their totem?"

"Some people have more than one." He decided not to go into too much detail. He'd always felt a connection to God's creatures, but had studied animal medicine in books. "They appear in visions or dreams. And sometimes they're just nearby, guiding and teaching you. You can feel it."

"What's your totem?"

In some tribes, asking someone about their spirit animal was inappropriate, but he didn't adhere to every tradition he'd read about. Besides, he had only recently remembered what nation he belonged to. He motioned to Tequila's terrarium. "Snake medicine."

Windy's jaw dropped and he realized she'd expected a different answer. "What gifts do snakes have?"

Tequila raised her head and Sky smiled. In a sense he communicated with Tequila on a telepathic level, accepting her gifts through his soul. "Snakes represent growth and change, the shedding of skin."

Suddenly Sky frowned, thinking about his black eye and bruised, aching body. How many times had he brawled in some honky-tonk bar? Hell, he hadn't changed a bit, shed his skin at all. "I guess I still have a lot to learn in that regard."

Rather than initiate that fight with Hank, he should have gotten Lucy's number and given it to Edith. The old lady would have been glad to help. Edith dedicated plenty of time to women's shelters. Maybe he'd cruise up to that dusty California town on his next day off and snoop around. Somebody might give him some information about Lucy. And while he was at it, he'd call the local police station about the vandalism and see if they had any leads. He'd feel a lot better if they caught those vandals. It would be hard to leave in three months if that wasn't settled.

Windy interrupted Sky's thoughts with a disturbing question. "Are hawks one of your totem animals, too?"

Oh, hell. He wished he'd never shattered that glass in front of her. "I don't know. I've just been seein' them lately." Having nightmares about them, too. He considered his nocturnal visions nightmares rather than dreams because the hawk always appeared with his son, and the boy was always crying.

Still perched on the end of the leather recliner, she posed another question. "What do hawks represent? What's their medicine?"

Feeling stiff, Sky moved from the floor to the couch. If she intended to keep this conversation going, then he needed to find himself a comfortable position. He sat next to her packages and stretched his legs. "Hawks are messengers."

Her eyes widened, and he could see the psychology wheels turning in her head. "Is that why that hawk upset you this morning? Did you think it was trying to send you a message?"

Yeah, a message that he was a jerk who had abandoned his kid. Irritated, he elbowed one of the packages, rustling the bag. "Hell, I don't know. I learned most of this medicine stuff from books. I'm not an authority."

"We don't have to talk about it right now," she said, clearly aware of his agitation, "but I have the feeling you know a lot more than any book could ever tell you."

Oh, right. That we-don't-have-to-talk-about-it-right-now

ploy was a tactic shrinks had used on him before. Did she think a guy with amnesia hadn't been grilled by psychiatrists and psychologists alike? Hell, they'd teamed up on him when he'd come out of that coma. Them and the cops. A possible runaway with a fake ID and no memory had intrigued them all, and now Windy had caught the fever sixteen years later.

"So when are you gonna unload all this kitchen junk you bought?" he asked, anxious to get rid of her so he could watch TV.

Five minutes later they ended up in the kitchen together. Like a fool he'd offered to help rather than avoid her sweet vanilla scent and annoying questions. She'd lugged her purchases down the hall and he'd watched her backside sway, thinking she had a cute little rear. But after she'd tossed that Lady Godiva mane over her shoulder, he'd given in and panted right after her.

"I appreciate your help," she said, "but I don't want you to push yourself. Those bruises need time to heal."

Sky drew his eyebrows together, wondering if his black eye looked as awful to her as it did to him. "I'm fine. Let's just get this done."

By the time they started unpacking bags and boxes, Sky fumed. What was it about this woman that had him behaving like a tortured kid with a crush? Was it her tender concern? Her unadorned beauty? A little of both, he suspected, thoroughly disgusted with himself.

Windy stood at the counter and attempted to open a small appliance box with a paring knife. Her unpracticed hand moved clumsily across the sealed flaps.

Sky reached for the box, then removed a pocket knife from his jeans. One quick slice opened it. Silent and sullen, he proceeded to open the rest of the boxes. She'd bought casserole dishes, serving platters, red-and-white dishes that matched the kitchen decor. There were other things, too, practical and impractical items like a blender and a food processor. He'd never understood what purpose a food processor served.

Windy chatted easily. "Edith made fried dough. She wanted

me to bring some home for you, but I didn't think they would keep well in my car while I was at the mall. It was so hot today. I'll get them later.''

"I can go to Edith's house myself. She lives only a couple blocks away.'' A sugary snack sounded good right about now. He'd upped his sweet intake since he'd quit smoking. Come to think of it, a cigarette sounded even better. He reached for the crumpled pack he kept in his pocket.

Windy cocked her head. "What are you doing?''

Another damn question, he thought. "What the hell does it look like I'm doing? I'm organizing the kitchen, for crying out loud.''

She eyed the cigarette pack in his hands. "Edith told me before you moved in here that you quit smoking. I don't allow smoking in my home.''

And he wouldn't allow himself to fall for some nosy little blonde. "I did quit.''

"Then what are you doing with those?''

He shot her a seething look. He sure as hell didn't intend to explain his nonsmoking method. She wouldn't understand that fingering a pack of cigarettes kept the craving in check. Besides, a man had a right to do things his own way without being interrogated. "Stay out of my business, Windy.''

"Your smoking in my house is my business,'' she snapped back.

This time her temper didn't strike him as cute, hissing kitten or not. "You're annoying, you know that?''

"And you're being a jerk. You don't mind having a woman around as long as you can eyeball her like she's a piece of meat. But the minute she speaks her mind, she's annoying.'' Windy clanked her new dishes. "I don't need this. I've been nothing but nice to you since you moved in.''

Nice to him? She'd been driving him mad with lust. Why in the hell did she think he'd been eyeing her like a piece of meat?

In a stubborn gesture, Sky sat at the table and crossed his

arms. "What you've been doing is sticking your nose in where it doesn't belong."

Windy tossed her head in an angry female fashion, and a bolt of desire shot through Sky. He had to stay mad—mad enough to keep himself from pulling her into his arms. Crushing his mouth against hers. Tangling his hands in her hair. Damn her, anyway.

Windy narrowed her eyes. "Well, do you smoke or don't you?"

As Sky leaned back, the chair teetered on two legs. Windy had the urge to knock him flat on his behind. The gorgeous, pigheaded male.

"I told you I quit." He shoved the crumpled pack back into his pocket.

She decided not to ask him why he carried cigarettes if he didn't smoke. He would probably just call her nosy. Besides, the real problem wasn't his wavering tobacco habit. His amnesia troubled him—not what he'd forgotten, but what he remembered. She knew something from his past had surfaced, something he didn't want anyone else to know about.

"You should talk about what's bothering you, Sky. I'm a good listener."

He rose from the table and began lining the shelves with the paper she'd bought, surprising her with his efficiency. Although still visibly angry, he measured, cut and peeled away the backing without missing a beat. "Don't start with that psychology bull. Just because I lost my memory doesn't mean you have to treat me like one of your patients."

Windy shoved the empty cartons and torn wrappers into a trash bag. "I'm not a practicing psychologist yet. What I am is a preschool teacher, and at the moment you're acting more immature than one of my students."

He cursed and all but ignored her. They worked side by side in agitated silence, determined to finish what they had started. Sky, Windy surmised, had too much pride to storm off before the task was done.

Over an hour later, when each paper-lined shelf boasted a thorough reorganization, Sky headed for the front door.

Now he's storming off, she thought, making his dramatic exit.

He jangled his keys in a childish attempt to get her attention. "I'm goin' to the market. I need some cereal for breakfast tomorrow."

Windy watched him go, wondering if that meant he didn't want her shopping or cooking for him. Well, fine and dandy. Big overgrown baby. He could clog his arteries with junk food. What did she care? While he poured milk on his chocolate crunchies or whatever he ate, she'd be making herself a mouthwatering breakfast, spicing the kitchen with a healthy, home-cooked aroma.

Frustrated, she retreated to her room, curled up in bed, and told herself what she needed was a short stress-relieving nap. She closed her eyes. Why waste her time stewing over Sky? At the moment he didn't deserve her empathy, or her well-intentioned concern.

Hours later Windy rose to discover she'd slept the afternoon away, not to mention most of the night. The alarm clock read 2:05 in bold red numbers. She peered through the eyelet curtains into a void of darkness. Now what was she supposed to do? Two in the morning wasn't exactly the rise-and-shine hour, but her growling stomach reminded her that she'd missed dinner. Maybe a cup of warm milk would cure the rumbling.

She turned on the light and stared at her reflection in the mirrored closet door. Good heavens. Her dress looked like, well, as if she'd slept in it. And her hair... She managed a weary smile and ran her fingers through her worst, and possibly best, feature. Spiral curls and long waves dueled for dominance.

She hated it; Sky loved it.

Windy studied her tousled reflection. What did Sky see when he looked at her? He called her Pretty Windy. Was that just part of his flirtatious nature to nickname women, or did he actually find her that appealing?

He found her sexually appealing, that much she knew. Like a shooting star, desire sparkled in those blue eyes, clearly reflecting unfulfilled wishes.

Curious, Windy checked her own sleepy eyes. Oh, Lord. The same impossible wish stared back at her. The same hopeless need. A need she would never act upon. No summer flings, she reminded herself, changing into a nightgown.

When her stomach growled again, she cleared her mind and headed for the bathroom to wash off remnants of yesterday's makeup and brush her teeth. By the time the peppermint taste faded, she would be sipping a cup of warm milk.

Five minutes later, feeling fresh and moisturized, Windy padded down the hall toward the kitchen. The house was dark but for the reddish glow from the snake's cage. She ignored an ominous chill and moved on.

When she flipped the kitchen light switch, her heart dived for her throat. A colorful bouquet sat on the table, nothing fancy, just a variety of posies wrapped in green cellophane. Beside them was a scrap of white paper. Windy inched forward and reached for the note.

I knocked on your door, but you didn't answer.
Sorry I acted like a jerk.

Sky

Lifting the bouquet, she hugged it to her chest and smiled. Still smiling, she filled a copper vase with water and arranged the flowers as a centerpiece. Fingering the delicate petals, she closed her eyes and imagined Sky at the market, cereal box in hand, stopping in front of the floral display. Her smile widened. He probably scowled at the bouquet before wrapping his big, calloused hands around it. What an incredible picture he must have made. Woman's intuition told her Sky had never bought flowers before.

Windy opened her eyes and pushed the image away. Dear God. What if she fell in love with him? Sky would be gone in three months.

Think logically, she told herself. It would never happen. They were wrong for each other, as different as the sun and the moon, Venus and Mars. Someday the right man would come along: a professional man, someone who wanted a wife and children.

She looked at the lively bouquet. As long as she lived, she would never forget Skyler or his touching apology. One day she would rock her granddaughter on her knee and tell the child about a handsome prince she once knew. A quiet laugh escaped. An off-beat prince with a crooked grin, dusty cowboy boots and a black eye.

The cup of milk forgotten, Windy sighed. Before Sky moved on, she had to help him. She couldn't live with herself if he continued to suffer. She would lie awake at night and worry.

This summer was their summer, she decided. They would spend every waking moment together. In three months they would part ways, and Sky would be emotionally stronger. Hopefully strong enough to face his past and the memories that disturbed him.

Pleased with her plan, Windy shut down the kitchen and stepped into the hall, using the snake's red light to guide her. And then she stopped and turned to look into the living room, praying her eyes deceived her.

No deception. The screened top on the snake's cage was askew, the glass enclosure empty. Once again Tequila had escaped.

Five

Windy stood in Sky's room, nervously twisting her hair. Squinting in the dark, she made her way to his dresser, then bumped her knee on the wood. She withheld a complaint and turned on the small brass lamp.

Sky stirred, his long body draped in a crisp white sheet. His hair tumbled over his pillow and half covered his face.

"Are you awake?" she asked, sensing he had heard her stumbling around.

He opened his eyes. "Am I dreaming? I must be. The woman standing beside my bed has to be a dream. She looks like an angel." He pushed his hair away from his face. "Hmm. She must have lost her wings. Lost her way, too. Never thought an angel would visit me." He peered at the clock and smiled. "Especially at this hour."

Windy didn't feel the least bit ethereal. "Tequila's not in her cage."

His pupils dilated, adjusting to the light. "Damn. So much for dreams. Thought you came in here to ravish me."

Although she recognized the teasing glint in his eyes, it didn't calm her anxiety. "I'm sorry to bother you, but I'm afraid to go back to my room. I went to the kitchen to get a glass of milk and I left my bedroom door open. When I saw that Tequila wasn't in her cage, I got a little worried that she might have gone into my room." Windy kept her arms crossed, hugging the chill. The snake being loose scared the death out of her. "Does she ever hide in bedrooms?"

"Sometimes." He sat up and winced as though his bruised muscles ached.

She avoided his gaze, feeling foolish about her fears. "I know snakes are your animal totem, but they still give me the creeps. Will you go look for Tequila?"

He sighed. "Did you leave your closet door open?"

She nodded. "My closet's jam packed and there're some open boxes under my bed, too. Lots of places for her to hide."

"Hell, she might be in your bed rather than under it. Tequila loves warm places." He shot her a mischievous grin. "And I've got a feeling your body could warm a bed."

"Don't you dare flirt with me. Not now." The last thing she needed was to envision that beast coiled in a tight ball under her covers, just waiting to strike.

"Sorry. I was just trying to defuse the situation." He groaned and pushed the pillow behind his back. "It's the middle of the night, I'm tired and sore, and it might take hours to find her. I'd much rather search in the morning. I'll go sleep on the couch and you can sleep in here."

Windy looked around suspiciously. "What if she's in here? Your door was open, too."

"Didn't consider that possibility."

He propped a second pillow behind him. His chest was bare, but the sheet had fallen below his waist, exposing the gray sweat shorts he seemed to favor.

"What should I do?" she asked herself as much as him.

"Well…" Thoughtful, Sky gazed up at the ceiling.

"Well, what?" she asked impatiently.

"If you're that scared," he began, then paused to study his fingernails.

"Dang it, Sky. You know I'm scared."

He expelled a heavy breath. "Okay, well…" He paused this time to search her face, then rushed his next words. "You could always sleep with me."

Windy's muscles tightened as her features turned to stone, making her feel like a statue etched in shock. "In the same bed?" she asked, wondering how she managed to move her mouth.

"It's the only solution I can think of. And I promise to behave."

Windy stared, her mouth still agape. He had called her an angel, yet the smile on his face appeared almost saintly. Almost. If he were a celestial being, he'd wear a halo the same way he wore a smile—lopsided.

A crooked angel. Just her luck. "Maybe we could stay up all night and watch TV," she suggested. "There's probably an old Western on."

"No way. I have to be fresh in the morning. We're rehearsing a new act."

Her thoughts strayed. "You're going to fall off horses in your condition?" His chest and stomach still looked like a road map of pain.

He shrugged. "Don't have a choice. Besides, it's not that bad."

She begged to differ since she'd caught him wincing earlier, but she had a more pressing issue to contend with. "No all-night TV, huh?"

"No, but I swear, Windy, if you sleep here, I won't try a thing."

Rather than respond, she assessed the bed and the man in it. The king-size bed was made up with white cotton sheets, a downy white blanket and a thick, quilted comforter. The man, an abundance of unrestrained black hair, too much brawn and a boyish glint in those azure-colored eyes.

It was him or the snake.

She couldn't ask Sky to sleep on the floor; the man was recovering from a beating. And she certainly didn't want to sleep on the floor; that slimy snake might crawl on her. And if she slept alone somewhere, she wouldn't have Sky's protection.

Besides, what harm was there in sleeping next to him? It wasn't as though anything would actually happen. She trusted him, but what was more important, she trusted herself. And although she hated to admit it, there was that curious side of her, the feminine part that wondered what it would feel like to share his bed, even platonically.

"Here's the deal," she said, trying to sound calmer than she felt. "We'll put pillows between us, and you'll have to sleep on top of the blanket. That way we won't accidentally…bump into each other."

He nodded, almost too eagerly, and Windy's stomach unleashed a hundred winged creatures. Goodness, she was actually going to sleep with him.

It took six pillows, two sheets and an extra blanket to transform the king-size bed into a sleeping fort. Windy bristled every time she glanced over at Sky. He peeked over the pillow barrier, grinning devilishly. Dang him, he probably knew how curious she was and found her inexperience amusing.

She crossed her arms and glared at him. "I'm glad you're enjoying this."

"Sorry," he apologized quickly and closed his eyes.

Windy inched closer to the bed. Him and that wicked grin. "You'll look for Tequila first thing in the morning, right?"

"Yep. First thing."

Staying as close to the edge as possible without falling off, Windy slipped under the covers and checked the pillow reinforcement. Against her better judgment, she turned off the brass lamp and lay in the darkness, listening to his shallow breaths.

How long would she stay awake, conscious of his presence? This was far too intimate. Talking, flirting, even arguing was easier than this awkward silence. His masculine, woodsy scent drifted to her nostrils, stimulating her senses. Somehow she didn't imagine him grinning anymore. His breathing had quickened as though he found her scent just as arousing. So much for feminine curiosity.

"Windy?"

"Hmm?"

"I'm sorry Tequila's been causing you so much trouble."

Windy peered over the pillows at him. Sharp angles and smooth planes prominently outlined his regal profile. A flowing curtain of black hair cloaked his broad shoulders. Even shadowed in the pitch of night, Sky looked majestic.

"I know how important Tequila is to you," she said, tiny bumps prickling her skin. "But I don't think I'll ever get used to having a snake loose in the house."

"I've never understood why people hate reptiles," Sky responded. "Even before I remembered what tribe I was from, I'd felt this connection to snakes. And then when I read about the Creeks, I discovered how important snakes were to their folklore."

He sounded happy to share a piece of his newfound culture, so Windy relaxed and listened.

"The Creeks believe in a mythical creature called tie snakes. Supposedly these friendly reptiles live in towns beneath the waters of creeks and swamps. Occasionally they capture someone and show them a good time. Word is, tie snakes are quite hospitable."

She smiled. "Have you ever been captured?"

He laughed. "Not that I can recall, but coming from a guy with amnesia that isn't saying much." His laughter faded softly as he turned toward her. "You know, Tequila's not a tie snake, but she's friendly. And smart, too. You should give her a chance."

Windy grimaced, grateful for the darkness. "Why did you name her Tequila?"

Leaning on one elbow, he chuckled softly. "She's from Mexico. At the time I got her, the only Spanish word I knew was Tequila."

"What is she again?"

"A boa constrictor."

Right. A boa constrictor. They strangle their prey. Now she could envision herself being strangled by a friendly, intelligent, Spanish-speaking snake.

"Can't you lock her cage, keep her in somehow?" Windy asked, unconsciously raising a hand to her throat.

"I guess I'll have to, at least until you get used to her. You know, most of the time she's content to stay put. I think she escaped tonight to get your attention. I think she wants you to notice her."

Windy smiled in spite of herself. She had noticed Tequila all right, noticed the enormous beast was missing. When she replayed the scene in her mind, her heart skipped a guilty beat. In all the snake chaos, she had forgotten to thank Sky for the flowers.

She gazed up at the ceiling, at the shadows playing across the wood beams. Moonlight shimmered through the window, creating a romantic ambience. A man had given her flowers and now she lay beside him in bed. For one silly, dreamy moment, she felt married.

"Sky?"

"Yeah?"

"Thank you for the flowers. That meant a lot to me."

"Sure," he responded somewhat shyly, and she imagined him ducking his head, even blushing a little.

When the silence that followed became too intimate, she pushed one of the center pillows toward him and groped for something to say. "So you really quit smoking?"

He pushed back, laughing a little. "Yeah, but I always keep a pack handy. Knowing they're available helps curb the craving. I only quit a few months ago."

"Well, good for you. I'm sure your lungs are grateful."

"I don't know. It might be too late. I've got the feeling they're already as black as my soul."

She straightened the pillow. "Don't say things like that."

"Why not?" Sky shifted his weight, stirring the mattress.

"I haven't lived a particularly clean life, you know. My soul is full of sin."

Was he looking for atonement? Or was he warning the good girl to stay away from the bad boy? This good girl wants to help you, she thought. "You don't seem all that wicked to me."

"Ah, but remember, I'm part snake."

She sighed. Trust him to change the subject. "Did you have to bring up snakes again? Knowing Tequila is still out there hoping to get my attention isn't a comforting thought."

"She won't hurt you, honey, I swear. But if it makes you feel any better I'll have a talk with her in the morning."

Windy pulled the sheet up to her neck. "Tell her to leave me alone," she said, realizing how ridiculous her request sounded. Regardless of what Sky believed, that snake couldn't possibly communicate on an intelligent level.

He bent his body to see the clock. "It's late. We better get some sleep."

"Sleep," Windy echoed, closing her eyes.

An hour later Windy woke Sky with a start. She screamed frantically, thrashing and kicking.

"Windy!" Disoriented in the dark, he pushed through the scattered pillows to reach her. Hold her. Restrain her. "Shhh." He found her waist and pulled her to his chest. "You're dreaming."

Her body rocked his. "The snake," she whimpered. "She was here."

"No," Sky protested softly, stroking her hair. "It was just a dream."

"Don't leave me," she whispered, moonlight trapping her tortured eyes. "Please…I don't want to be alone."

"I won't leave you." Instinctively he drew her closer. Her heart pumped furiously, pushing against her rib cage. Against his. "Do you want me to turn on the light?"

Panic rose in her voice. "You said you wouldn't leave."

"I won't, honey." He leaned over, taking her with him as he flipped on the bedside lamp.

As Windy nuzzled his chest, her hands slid bonelessly down his back, caressing without intent. "So scared," she muttered.

Sky knew what it was like to have nightmares. He had the same one often enough. Hell, almost nightly. Somehow, though, he knew it wouldn't happen tonight, not with her beside him. Maybe that's why he had invited her into his bed so readily.

"Do you want to talk about it?" he asked.

"Not yet," she whispered.

Sky eased her to the bed and stroked her cheek, offering comfort. They felt good together, her curves, his muscles.

Windy stirred in his arms as though familiarizing herself with the consolation he provided. He kissed her forehead. "You all right now?"

She nodded, but made no attempt to move away. Maybe she thought they felt good together, too.

"I dreamed about Tequila."

"Tell me about it."

"I don't remember much. I think she was trying to talk to me, but I wouldn't listen. I was afraid she was going to strangle me. And there was a scarlet flame burning around me, too. A ring of fire. Tequila went right through it."

Sky bent his head to gaze at her. Her eyes were closed, thick lashes pressed against her cheekbones. Maybe she had no idea what her dream meant, but he did. "Tequila wasn't trying to hurt you, honey. She was offering you part of her medicine. Snakes are the keeper of fire. Fire energy brings passion and desire."

She opened her eyes. "I'm sorry, Sky, but I don't believe in animal medicine the way you do. My dream was about fear. I dreamed about Tequila because I'm afraid of snakes."

By denouncing Tequila's medicine, Windy was denying the fire, he thought. The heat between them. The hunger. He knew he should let it go, but he couldn't. "Don't psychologists believe in analyzing dreams?"

"Freud had his theories."

"And did Freud have a theory about what snakes represent?"

When Windy's cheeks colored, Sky smiled. He knew Freud's theory involved a specific part of the male anatomy. "You know as well as I do, Pretty Windy, your dream was not about fear."

Although she didn't respond, streaks of gold sparked her eyes. Her fire, he thought. His was in his loins now, growing rigid with desire.

Unable to stop himself, he skimmed his knuckles over her cheek. Her skin was soft and smooth. Luxuriously feminine.

As their gazes locked, she returned the touch, a tentative stroke that turned his mind blank and made his body grow harder. Suddenly the need to taste her clouded his vision. She looked so touchable beside him, all woman and as warm as the sun.

He lowered his head, felt her fingers move from his face to his hair, tangling gently. Was she urging him closer?

Sky swallowed. Seconds passed—torturous seconds of listening to the catch in her breath, the struggle of his own.

He shifted his weight, sliding his hands down the curve of her spine. Their mouths, inches apart, came together. She made a mewling sound, and his senses staggered. The kiss was neither chaste nor ravenous. It was, he decided, a smooth, slow dance. A mating. A shared exploration. An incredible sensation that slid from his body to hers then back again.

Sky groaned and deepened the kiss. She tasted like seduction, a blend of shyness and woman, sensuality and innocence.

As his blood pumped faster, he slid his hands into her hair, into those wild, tumbling locks. She licked his bottom lip, and his mind drifted to lovemaking—slick bodies, naked and aroused, joined in a warm, wet sinuous rhythm.

God, he wanted her.

No!

The unwelcome word sounded like an alarm in his head.

He had to stop himself before he went too far, took her where she might regret going.

Struggling to break the spell, Sky opened his eyes and ended the kiss, painfully removing his lips from hers.

Their gazes met in awkward silence, breaths unsteady, bodies much too close.

"I'm sorry," he managed in a hoarse whisper. "I shouldn't have done that. I promised to behave and…"

She pulled her hands away as though unsure of where to put them. "It's okay. I…we both…"

Her lips were still parted, he noticed, and goose bumps covered her arms.

"Are you cold?" he asked, knowing it wasn't a chill that caused her shiver but the erotic fever flowing through her veins. Her nipples pressed against the silk of her gown, blooming with feminine passion.

Instead of waiting for a response, he drew the quilt over her, shielding her from his hungry gaze. "I'll put the pillows back," he said, moving away from her. The blankets and pillows were in disarray, the bed resembling a lover's den. Instantly he began righting the bed, smoothing the blankets, stacking the pillows neatly between them.

She watched him, her gaze gliding over his body. "Are you sore?" she asked, looking beautifully dazed.

"A little." He avoided her eyes, the amber flames beckoning him. It was his need to be touched that pained him, not the bruises coloring his flesh. "All done," he said, dragging a sheet across his middle, over the swollen body part tenting his shorts.

"I'll get the light," she whispered, reaching for the lamp, darkening the room.

He nodded and closed his eyes as moonlight slipped into the room once again. God, how he wished he could hold her, bury his face in her hair and lull them both into a sweet, sensual slumber. At least then they could dream, he thought, of what could never be.

* * *

The next morning Windy found Sky on the patio, toying with the spoon in his cereal bowl. Steam rose from his coffee, twirling until it dissipated into the air. Dressed in threadbare jeans, black boots and a Stetson to match, he looked like a young rancher having breakfast in suburban California. The yard smelled of yesterday's mowed grass, Valencia oranges and an ancient avocado tree.

Seeing a man at the glass-topped table made her think of long summer weekends, barbecues, children and a happy marriage.

She stood silent for a moment, picturing herself in the setting. Her unruly hair was fastened with a blue ribbon that matched the flowers on her no-frills cotton dress. She wore minimal makeup: taupe eye shadow, one coat of dark-brown mascara, a hint of blush. The shine on her lips was honey-flavored gloss and the fragrance on her skin, vanilla perfume. She probably looked like what she was: a preschool teacher ready to begin her wonderful, harried day.

Sky had yet to notice her. He sat staring at his cereal as though the sugar-coated shapes could predict the future. The brim of his hat dipped low, shielding his eyes.

"Mind some company?" Windy asked, raising a container of lime yogurt. "I brought my own breakfast."

He lifted his head, taking in her appearance with a smile. "Sure. Have a seat."

She placed the yogurt, a paper napkin and a spoon on the tabletop, wondering what to say now. They had spent the night together, kissed each other passionately, but barely mumbled an audible hello when they rose from bed this morning. Virtually ignoring each other, Sky had searched for the snake while she showered and dressed. Of course, before she had even entered the bathroom, Sky had checked it thoroughly for Tequila's presence. Soon after that he'd found Tequila behind the sofa and banished the errant reptile to its cage, slipping a bolt into the lock to keep the snake inside.

Windy dipped into the yogurt and tried not to think about being in Sky's arms last night. Their kiss had made her feel the way she imagined a long, languorous night of lovemaking might feel—warm and secure. Sensual.

He glanced up from his soggy cereal and sent her heart askew. "Green yogurt?"

She swallowed a mouthful. "It tastes like key-lime pie."

"Really?" His eyes lit up.

"Do you want a bite?"

He cocked his head, checked the label, winced. "I don't know. Says it's fat free."

Windy laughed. "Everything good for you doesn't taste bad." How he maintained that lean, muscular physique was beyond her.

He scooted his chair closer. "Maybe just a little bite. But I'm warning you, if it's awful, I'm spitting it out."

She rolled her eyes at his childish comment, then dunked the spoon. Without thinking, she put it to his lips. When he opened his mouth, the intimacy of the moment seized her. The fire that had burned low in her belly last night returned—with a vengeance.

Their gazes met and held. His eyes, even the swollen one, sparkled in the morning light. "More, Pretty Windy. I like it."

Windy drew the spoon back. What he liked, she thought, was being fed, pampered by a woman. She prayed her hands wouldn't reveal her sudden anxiety by trembling. "There's another one in the fridge. I'll get—"

"No." He gripped her shoulder to keep her in place. "I only want a few bites. We can share."

They had already shared too much. A steam-filled bathroom, a romantic kiss, warm embraces. A bed. "Here." She handed him the spoon-ladled container. "Eat as much as you want. I'm not all that hungry."

He ate one small helping, then another. Windy sat like a voyeur and watched him open his mouth, place the spoon inside and swallow. As his neck muscles moved, she envisioned the yogurt sliding down his throat.

This was no way to deal with their attraction. And neither

was sleeping in the same bed with him. No matter what, she should *never* do that again.

"Are you sure you don't mind if I finish this?" he asked. "Hate to steal your breakfast."

"Go ahead." She checked her ponytail, grateful for something to do. A small breeze had kicked up, loosening several strands. "I usually snack with my kids. This morning we're having peanut butter crackers and bananas. It won't hurt me to skip breakfast."

His easy expression faltered. "They're not your kids, Windy, they're your students. Big difference."

"I didn't mean it literally. And for eight hours out of the day they are mine." Struggling to control her temper, she squared her shoulders. How dare he discredit the affection she felt for her students. "Why are children such a sore subject with you?"

His gaze shot up, as defensive as his tone. "I got nothing against kids. Fact is, Melissa is anxious to come over."

Curious, she leaned forward. "Really? Who's that?"

"Charlie's daughter." Clearly agitated, he shooed away a fly that buzzed near. "And for your information, she happens to like me."

"I'm sorry, I never meant to imply…" She studied his scowl, thinking how hard it made him look. There were times his face held none of its boyish appeal. "I'm looking forward to meeting Charlie's family."

"Yeah, they wanna meet you, too." He sipped his coffee then gazed into the cup. "You're the first woman I've ever lived with. They act like it's some big damn deal. I told 'em we're just roommates."

"Yes, we're just roommates," Windy agreed, wondering why that admission suddenly hurt.

Six

Nearly a week later Windy sat at the kitchen table, watching Sky devour Edith's apple pie while the three discussed his plan to locate a young woman named Lucy. Lucy, Windy learned, was the abused wife of one of the men with whom Sky had picked a fight.

"At first I thought it would be simple. You know, just head up to that little town and ask around," Sky said. "Check out the local supermarket, places like that. But then, I realized that would never do." He finished the dessert on his plate and reached for a frothy glass of milk. "If Lucy's husband got wind that another man was asking about her..." He let his statement hang in the cinnamon-spiced air, inviting shivers from his companions.

Women, Windy thought, always cringed at the mention of spousal abuse. Even Edith, who volunteered at a Christian shelter that housed victim after victim, had reacted strongly to his words. Clearly, abuse wasn't something a person got used to seeing.

Without commenting, Edith served Sky another slice of pie, her bifocals perched on the end of her nose. As usual, the elderly woman didn't have a hair or a thread out of place. Her navy skirt and white blouse looked freshly laundered and pressed to perfection. Windy assumed plying Sky with sweets made Edith feel better about what was sounding like a hopeless plan.

Windy had to admit Sky's gallant determination to rescue Lucy pleased and surprised her. It wouldn't be easy, though. Even if he found Lucy, the young woman might look upon his interest in her well-being as interference. She breathed a soft sigh. Windy knew firsthand how it felt to have someone reject the help you offered. Sky did it to her whenever she broached the subject of his troublesome memories.

"I shouldn't have provoked that fight," he said, "but all I could think about was how tiny and scared Lucy looked. Hank kept shoving her around, and then he refused to give her his car keys. And believe me, he was too drunk to drive."

"And the other man was Hank's brother?" Windy asked.

"Yeah. Both of 'em were big, ugly sons of a bi—"

"Skyler," Edith reprimanded. "Please watch your language. You're in the presence of ladies."

His gaze dropped, his chastised expression reminding Windy of an old-fashioned schoolboy who'd just had his knuckles rapped. "Sorry, ma'am. You, too, Windy."

She bit back a smile and picked up the conversation where it left off. "Sky, have you considered going back to that bar and offering to buy Hank a drink? Maybe apologize for the trouble you caused?"

"Wouldn't work. He'd throw a punch and ask questions later."

"Maybe not if you were standing there with a woman by your side. I have the feeling someone like Hank would enjoy watching you cower in front of a woman." Flashing her best smile, Windy fluffed her hair. "And I know just the woman. A future psychologist, no less."

His baby blues narrowed. "No way. You're not getting involved in this."

She protested. "Think about it. If Lucy's there, I could talk to her while you're humbling yourself to Hank."

Windy wanted the opportunity to put her healing skills to good use, and she needed a way to win Sky's trust, as well, to prove her competency. At times she thought he viewed her as nothing more than a little blond nuisance.

"No way," he said again, more firmly this time.

Edith came quickly to Windy's aid. "It's a good idea, Sky, and probably the only way for you to locate these people without calling attention to yourself. You said Hank was a regular at this bar." The older woman placed her hands on the table. "Even if Lucy isn't there, it would give you the opportunity to establish yourself in Hank's environment, and you'd be less threatening if you had a woman with you."

A scowl slashed across Sky's face, tightening his mouth and hooding his eyes. "I don't like it, but I catch your drift. Sooner or later we'd come across Lucy, and if I kept supplying Hank with beer, he'd get over his beef with me. Maybe even consider me one of his drinking buddies." He glanced at Windy. "And it's possible Lucy might need a woman to talk to."

"That's right." Edith found his hand and squeezed it. "But remember, this might not work out the way you want it to. Lucy may have a million excuses as to why she can't leave her husband."

"Yeah, but she's scared of him. I saw it in her eyes."

"Fear is often the reason women stay. If they leave they know the abuser will come after them. Being stalked is a frightening possibility."

"I understand." He turned to Windy, his expression grim. "Whadda ya say, pretty lady, wanna go barhopping tonight?"

Because a wave of excitement flooded her chest, she made an effort to appear calm. She had never been on a cloak-and-dagger mission before. "Why, cowboy, I thought you'd never ask."

* * *

Hank hadn't shown up at the first bar, so Sky and Windy headed to another one in the area, hoping to catch him there. Sky thought Windy had been a good sport at the last dive, trying her damnedest to fit in. She had sat at a corner table with him for two long hours, sipping ginger ale and avoiding direct eye contact with the bar's surly inhabitants.

"This place isn't as bad," she said, as they entered the Country Moose Bar and Grill.

Immediately, Sky scanned the room looking for Hank and Jimmy's ugly mugs, but didn't see either. "Yeah, it's all right," he said, thinking he'd been in a thousand joints just like this one.

A pool table sat in the left-hand corner, a jukebox in the right. The building was fairly large with scarred wood tables and cement floors sprinkled with sawdust. Experienced waitresses in skin-tight denim and Country Moose T-shirts served foaming beers and plates of greasy food. One tall redhead had tried to catch his eye on her way to the kitchen. Brassy and flirtatious, she used her abundant curves to her best advantage, thriving on the masculine attention she received. Sky knew the type well. He'd rolled in the proverbial hay with enough of them. Cocktail waitresses seemed to like him, but this one wouldn't be like the brunette in that trendy Burbank bar. This one wouldn't think twice about moving in on someone else's man.

Sky took Windy's hand and chose a table away from the redhead's station. He didn't want to be reminded of gritty sex in cheap motels. He might not be Windy's date, but he considered her a friend, a lady he wouldn't disrespect by ogling another woman.

Windy scooted her chair forward. "I take it Hank isn't here."

"No, but we can grab a bite while we wait. I'm pretty sure this was the name of the place he and Lucy had argued about. He wanted to come here, and she wanted to go home."

Windy handed Sky the lone menu on the table. "Not much to choose from."

The limited selection didn't surprise him. The Country Moose was more of a bar than a grill, offering items like jalapeño nachos and potato skins. Drinking food, he called it.

Their waitress appeared, a blonde with dark-brown roots and a bright smile. She complimented Windy on her "awesome" hair and told Sky he had "the coolest eyes." When she brought their drinks, she leaned on the table and flashed her pearly whites.

"You two look good together. People say that about me and my old man, too. He's a bartender." She lifted a pen to the order pad. "That's how we met."

Sky nodded indifferently. This gal's love life didn't interest him, but he appreciated the part about him and Windy looking good together. He didn't want anyone thinking they made an unusual pair. He had this awful fear Hank would see right through their ploy.

They ordered from the limited menu and sent the chatty waitress on her way. Sky considered stacking the appropriate amount of quarters on the pool table to signal his interest in a future game, but thought better of it. Windy didn't seem like the billiards type, and he needed to sit tight and keep an eye out for Hank or Jimmy. He didn't want to be caught off guard.

"This doesn't seem like the kind of place where someone could get into a brawl," Windy said. "The bouncer at the door was pretty big."

"Just because that last place was such a dive, don't let this one fool ya. Take a good look around, honey."

While Windy took his advice and studied the other patrons, he made his own assessment. Both the men and the women at the Country Moose exhibited a hard, feral edge—the kind that came from living on the wrong side of the tracks. Sky knew he fit in just fine. He figured Windy's wild locks had fooled their waitress into believing she was one of them. Good girls weren't supposed to have bedroom hair. Nature had played a trick on Pretty Windy.

She turned away from the hard-drinking crowd. "How did you find this area, anyway? It's certainly off the beaten path."

Sky reached for the beer he intended to nurse for as long as possible. He wanted to smell like Hank's favorite brew without actually being hammered. "I'm a drifter. Off the beaten path comes natural."

The waitress brought the potato skins they'd decided to share. "Last food call," she said. "Kitchen's getting ready to close."

"This will do us fine," Sky responded, knowing Windy would pick at the snack like a little bird. They had nothing in common, not even their appetites. For a girl who liked to cook, she didn't eat more than a thimbleful of food at a time.

While Windy removed bacon bits from a cheese-laden potato skin, Sky dipped his into a side of sour cream and watched the front door.

She sipped a tall cherry cola. "See anything interesting?"

"No." Sky dropped his guilt-ridden gaze in a hurry. The busty redhead had smiled at him from across the room, reminding him of the sexual itch he hadn't scratched in over eight months.

She fingered her straw, absently stirring her drink with it. "What about that red-haired waitress who keeps staring at you? Don't you think she's interesting?"

A corner of the cheesy potato wedge he'd been eating nearly stuck to the roof of his mouth. Was he that transparent or did Windy have eyes in the back of her head? "She's all right."

"A walking sex machine I'd say. Probably just your type."

He found himself grinning. For some odd reason the catty barb pleased him. "Jealous, Pretty Windy?"

She glanced away. "Your taste in women is none of my business. You and I are just roommates."

Roommates. Yeah, right. That enormous white lie had gone on long enough. "That's bull and we both know it. If our attraction were a chemistry set, we would have blown up the house by now."

She had the grace to laugh, even though an obvious case of nerves had set in. "Chemistry was my worst subject."

Because of all the sparks she must have caused, he decided,

wishing he could touch her hand, stroke each slender finger, rub his thumbs over the half-moons on her nails. She looked womanly tonight—tumbling hair, a top that exposed her navel, great-fitting jeans. She'd tried to dress for honky-tonk barhopping, but he knew she was the kind of girl mothers wanted their sons to marry. The kind of girl a low-down cowboy had no business dreaming about.

He filled his lungs with air, forced himself release it. "I think there's something I should tell you."

Her caramel eyes grew big and doelike. "I'm listening."

He moved his chair next to hers, close enough to protect their privacy. "You don't have to worry about me making a pass at you."

"A pass?"

"Yeah." His tongue felt heavy, as if he'd swallowed a bucket of wet sand. "As in I won't try to take you to bed." When his palms turned sweaty, he rubbed them against his jeans. "I gave up sex. I've been celibate for over eight months."

Clearly startled, her jaw went lax. "Why? You seem like such a sexual person."

He wished he could tell her some outrageous lie, such as he was on a spiritual quest that forbade him from physical pleasure. But she deserved to know the truth. Especially since she was the one playing havoc with his hormones. "I'm a user, that's why. I haven't cared about the women I've slept with." He pulled a hand through his hair, then remembered he'd banded it into a ponytail. "And believe me, there's been a lot. Too many." Not that he'd been completely stupid. He had used protection. Every time but one, he thought wryly. He couldn't have fathered a child if he'd used protection then.

She cast her sweet, limpid eyes on his. "Are you punishing yourself, Sky?"

Was he? Yes, he thought, for leaving his child, for not knowing how to make a commitment. "I don't have it in me to get emotionally involved with a woman, but on the other hand, sleeping around feels wrong. I figured if I steered clear of sex, there wouldn't be any morning afters to feel bad about.''

She grazed his cheek in a warm, comforting gesture. ''I think I understand why you made that choice, but don't sell your emotional capabilities short. You're a kind and decent man. You have so much to offer. All you need is the right woman.''

Sky closed his eyes and let her touch wash over him. She had a healer's hands, and a healer's heart, too. She had called him kind. Decent. If only he had the courage to tell her everything. But if he did, she'd hate him. Windy had dedicated her life to children, and he'd walked out on his own flesh and blood. She wouldn't forgive him that.

He opened his eyes, looked right at her. ''Happily ever after. The right woman, the perfect man. I don't think that fairy tale exists.''

She removed her hand from his cheek and reached for her drink. ''I believe in it. In fact, I've based some important decisions around that theory.'' She sipped the soda and smiled a telling smile. ''I'm still waiting for the right man.''

Still waiting for the right man. Coming from Windy, he had a pretty good idea what that meant. He kept his voice pitched low. A noisy, crowded bar was a hell of a place for this conversation. ''Are you saying you've never had sex?''

She nodded. ''Does that surprise you?''

Yes. No. ''Are you holding out for your wedding night?''

Her smile turned wistful. ''Not necessarily, although I've always thought that would be romantic.''

An ache that he figured had to be envy shot through his gut. Some lucky guy would get to make love to Pretty Windy, carry her to bed, remove her flowing white gown, cover that smooth, luxurious skin with his hands. ''You deserve the American dream. A husband, kids, a house with a garden. Whatever you want.''

''Thank you, but don't forget about a career. Married women have careers these days.''

''Yeah.'' He pictured her married to another professional.

A doctor, maybe. Someone smart and successful. A guy who didn't come with emotional baggage. A guy who loved kids. He'd be good-looking, too—the clean-cut sort who felt comfortable in a suit and tie. Sky lifted his beer. He hated the guy already.

She sat a little straighter, both hands around her glass. "I'm glad we talked about this. I think it will take some of the pressure off that chemistry between us. What can happen, right? I'm a virgin, and you're celibate."

"Yeah. We're quite a pair." Realizing how close they were, he moved his chair away. Her virginity and his self-imposed celibacy hadn't changed a thing. Their attraction remained, crackling between them like a frayed wire. Electrocution was only a heartbeat away.

"We can concentrate on being friends," she said. "It's possible for a man and a woman to be friends."

Who was she trying to convince, him or herself? "You want another soda?" he asked, noticing her empty glass.

She nodded. "Yes, please. It's hot in here."

"Yeah." Heat seemed to follow them, flow through their bodies like a warm, rhythmic current. Turning to look for the waitress, he caught sight of a surprise. His heart skipped a beat. "Hank just arrived. And he's got Lucy with him."

Windy took one look at the couple in the doorway and felt sick. Hank stood taller than she had expected with tree-trunk arms squeezed into a sweat-stained T-shirt. When he ambled forward, the dingy jeans slung low on his hips strained to make room for a protruding belly. His face, unshaven and ruddy, was framed by dark-brown hair cropped close to his scalp.

Lucy, pale and thin, clung to his arm as though her life depended on his generosity. A lit cigarette burned in her hand, a column of ashes gathering on its tip. Her clothes were clean but faded; her wiry, red hair clean but faded, too.

They headed to a table near the jukebox, where it appeared the bouncer had told Lucy to extinguish her cigarette. Unlike the previous bar, the Country Moose enforced the California smoking ban.

Sky signaled their waitress and ordered Windy another soda, then pointed to Hank and Lucy. "Will you tell that couple's waitress that their tab is on me."

"That big ape a friend of yours?" the blonde asked.

"I owe him a drink," Sky responded diplomatically.

"It's your money." The blonde turned on her booted heel and disappeared.

Sky and Windy exchanged a look. "What do we do now?" she asked.

"Wait and see what happens. I'd rather Hank approach us than the other way around."

She drew a deep breath. "I wasn't expecting Lucy to be here. Were you?"

"No. I guess a part of me was hoping she left him that night. That she would have taken her kids and split." He sipped the domestic beer. "Why do you think he brings her to these dives? I thought his type preferred to party without their wives."

Windy pushed away the platter of half-eaten potatoes. "Most abusive men are extremely possessive. If Hank takes Lucy with him, he can keep an eye on her. Control her, in a sense."

Sky lifted his beer again, a shadow of guilt deepening the shade of his eyes. "I'll bet he was mad as hell about what I did the other week. Probably took it out on her."

Windy reached for his hand, squeezed it. "You can't blame yourself for someone else's actions."

They held hands and stared at each other, waiting and wondering what Hank would decide to do. Sky's touch spread through Windy like melting butter on warm bread: rich, thick and comforting. For a man who claimed he couldn't give of himself emotionally, he spent plenty of time protecting others. First Edith and now Lucy. And Lord only knew how many in between.

Their waitress brought Windy's soda. "Here you are." Motioning toward Hank, she spoke to Sky. "He says he doesn't want you buying him drinks. And he wasn't very polite about it, either."

Sky watched her go, then cursed. "Well, that backfired, didn't it?" He stole a quick glance at Lucy, who sat beside her husband with her shoulders narrowed. "Now we'll never get to talk to Lucy."

Windy reached for Sky's hand. "We'll find a way, okay?"

"How? We both know Hank will never let her out of his sight." He pulled away, the disappointment in his eyes turning to despair. "You know what I think?" He closed his vacant eyes, opened them. "I think that Lucy doesn't have a family, that there's nobody who cares."

Windy hesitated to respond. Second-guessing Lucy's background seemed unproductive at this point. There was no cut-and-dried profile on abuse victims. "It's hard to say. There could be a hundred different case scenarios. Her family could live out of state, or they could be involved in her daily life, but she refuses to let them intervene."

Sky shook his head. "No. I'm telling you. There isn't anyone. She's an orphan."

An *orphan*. The word choice set off an alarm bell in Windy's head. Adults rarely thought of other adults as orphans. Unless of course… "Is that what happened to you, Sky? Did you lose your family?"

The despair returned to his eyes, deeper this time, more intense. "I…" He rocked his chair, looked away, then back again. "Yeah, I think so, but I'm not positive."

She prayed he wouldn't sink into himself, into the pain she saw. This was the first time he had spoken honestly about his past. "What is it you remember?"

"Even though the details are vague, I know I lived with other people's families when I was a kid."

Foster care, Windy thought, her heart aching. Of course there were good foster families, people who cared, but being shifted from home to home took its emotional toll on a child.

"If you were a ward of the state, that means tracing your roots may be possible. We could contact Social Services—"

"A ward of what state?" he asked.

"Whatever state you're—" Her aching heart dropped to the floor. "You don't know what state you're from, do you?"

"No." His voice remained quiet, lonely and distant. "And Reed isn't my real last name. I don't remember what my true name is, but I know it's not Reed." While he spoke, he glanced back at Hank and Lucy periodically, apparently still concerned about the frail young woman he assumed was a fellow orphan. "I am Skyler, though. That much I know. You see, I have what's called selective memory. Some things are clear, others a complete washout."

Selective memory wasn't much to go on. "Edith said it's possible you'll remember everything someday," she commented, not knowing what else to say. If he had been orphaned, then he had no one, she thought. No one but Charlie, Edith and herself. In that dawning moment Windy didn't want to let him go. Ever.

When their waitress returned, they both refused another drink, then sat quietly amid the vast, noisy bar, country tunes continuously wailing on the jukebox.

A morose thirty minutes later, Sky rocked his chair then grabbed Windy's hand. "Look," he said, his eyes suddenly bright. "I think Lucy's headed for the ladies' room."

Windy watched the young woman dart across the room, dodging other patrons in her quest. She squeezed Sky's hand and rose. "Hank can't follow her in there," she said, hope forming her smile, "but I certainly can."

Seven

Hours later and unable to sleep, Windy fixed herself a cup of herbal tea. Approaching Lucy hadn't been easy. The other woman had seemed nervous and flighty. And she'd refused the name and number of the abuse shelter, claiming, "I don't need any help."

Their hasty conversation had ended with Windy offering Lucy her personal number. "I'm listed in Burbank as W. Hall," she'd told the redhead. "There's no address, but you can get the number from information. Call me if you ever need to talk."

Windy sweetened her tea, then left the kitchen. Lucy had referred to Sky as "Good Sam with the pretty blue eyes." What a fitting description, she thought, a smile tugging her lips. Good Sam. Kind-hearted Skyler.

When she passed Sky's door and heard his voice she stopped, unable to decipher his words. He must be inviting her to his room to resume their conversation. After returning home from the bar, they had discussed Lucy at length, wondering and worrying about the frail young woman.

Since the door was slightly ajar, she pushed it open farther, then stared in confusion. Sky sat on his bed, holding a teddy bear at arm's length.

"Sky?"

He looked up and dropped the toy in a near panic. "Damn it, Windy. Haven't you ever heard of knocking?"

"I…" She glanced at the stuffed animal. The fuzzy brown bear appeared old. Tattered and worn, frayed ears sat atop its misshapen head while both eyeballs hung by a thread. Even its smile seemed tired. "I'm-sorry. I didn't mean to intrude. I thought—" she glanced at the bear again "—I thought you knew I was in the hall and that you were talking to me."

Clearly embarrassed, he frowned. "Well, I wasn't."

She stood awkwardly, clutching her warm teacup. She couldn't go back to bed. The discarded teddy bear wouldn't let her. "Is he important?" she asked, determining the bear's gender by the faded blue ribbon tied around its neck.

Sky's frown deepened. "Yeah. Sorta. I've had him forever, I guess."

Intrigued, she inched closer. Apparently the tired little bear was a link to his childhood. "A lot of people keep mementos from their past," she said, hoping to ease his discomfort.

"Do you?"

She sipped her tea, nodded. "I save lots of things." She had even kept one of the flowers he had given her, pressed in her Bible to remember him by.

He pushed a stray hair off his forehead. He wore his usual sleeping attire: gray sweat shorts and bare bronzed flesh. "I'll bet you don't talk to stuffed animals, though."

She smiled. It had seemed odd to see a grown man conversing with a tattered little bear. "I don't have amnesia, either. If talking out loud helps you to remember—"

"It does," Sky admitted quickly, then picked up the stuffed toy and held it out to Windy. "I think his name's Jesse."

Pleased that he had invited her into an emotional part of his past, she placed her tea on the nightstand and took the bear. "What makes you think that's his name?"

"Every time I look at him the name Jesse pops into my mind. I think I used to talk to him when I was a kid. You know, when I lived in foster care." He squared his shoulders. "I guess I was just trying to remember what I used to say to him. Pretty dumb, huh?"

"No. Not at all." She traced the frayed seam on Jesse's lopsided head, resisting the urge to hug the inanimate creature to her breast. In her mind's eye, she could see Sky as a child, beautiful, alone and afraid, whispering secrets to his teddy bear. "Objects from our past can make us feel closer to our memories, to people we've known, places we've been. And in your case I think that's extremely important."

He shrugged, and Windy wondered if he recalled anything about his biological family. He might not be an orphan in the sense that his parents had actually died. He may have been abandoned, an emotional devastation that would make a child feel orphaned. Windy released a heavyhearted breath. Although her father had died, she knew kids whose dads had disappeared, neglecting their emotional and financial obligations to their children. Abuse came in many forms and, sadly enough, mothers as well as fathers were capable of it.

Windy sat on the edge of Sky's bed and searched for a question that wouldn't sound as though she were prying too deeply. His eyes had glazed, as though exposing his vulnerability had been a mistake. "Does Edith know about your foster care memories?"

"No. I told you because of Lucy. Otherwise, I probably wouldn't have mentioned it. I mean, what does it matter?"

Apparently it mattered enough for him to pull Jesse out of the closet, or wherever he stored the tattered teddy bear. "Your past is important, Sky."

"I know. But until I remember who I really am, I can't look for anyone, or…" He moved to the side of the bed, planted his feet on the floor. "Talkin' about this is a waste of time."

Windy couldn't let it go that easily, not after what he'd said.

"Who would you look for? Do you think your parents might still be alive?" She searched his gaze as he came toward her. "Not all kids in foster care are orphaned."

He grabbed Jesse out of her arms. "Damn it. Am I a case study to you or a person? Half the time I feel like you're picking my brain for research or something."

She watched him jam the poor little bear into the bottom dresser drawer. A part of her felt maternal toward his childhood toy. And toward him, she thought—for the lonely boy he once was, the guarded man he'd become. "That's not what I'm doing. If I ask you a lot of questions, it's because I care. I know something is troubling you from your past. I want to help."

"Then ease up, okay? Quit trying to be my psychologist. I've been down that road before." He paced the hardwood floor on silent feet, his muscles taut yet lean. For a big man, he moved with a loose, fluid gait. "And of course something's bothering me. I have amnesia. I don't know where I was born, or even what my last name is. Stuff like that would bug most people."

"You're right. I'm sorry." What he needed was a friend, not a Ph.D. She patted a corner of the bed. "Sit with me a minute."

He parked himself beside her, crossed his arms stubbornly. "Why? What do you want?"

"Nothing much." She smiled, hoping to pull one out of him. "I like your cologne. I just wanted you close so I could smell you."

He gave her more than a smile. His eyes sparkled like freshly mined diamonds, rough yet beautiful. "Are you flirting with me, Pretty Windy?"

Was she? No. Not deliberately. "Why would you assume that?"

He tapped the end of her nose. "'Cause I ain't wearing any cologne."

"You're not?" Windy inhaled, certain she detected traces of leather and musk. "Then it must be your room."

A room that reflected the cowboy who slept there. The black Stetson he favored sat atop the dresser, along with a set of pointy spurs and a tooled leather belt. The open closet depicted various shades of denim, small boxes crammed with unknown items and a familiar pair of dusty black boots. Although the room wasn't messy, it wasn't tidy, either. The clothes he'd worn earlier were piled in the only free corner.

She looked back at him and shivered. He had allowed his finger to slide from her nose, to her lips, then beneath her chin in one gentle motion. The urge to kiss his finger stunned her. Discussing their attraction was supposed to make moments like this easier. Less sexual.

"Do you realize how many times you've been in my bedroom?" he asked.

Too many, she wanted to say. "Three."

He nodded. "First time you were wearing a towel, the second a pink nightgown." Smiling, he fingered her pajama top. "And now this."

Her mind went suddenly blank, and she glanced down at her chest to refresh her memory. Good grief. Cat-and-mouse pajamas with no bra and erect nipples. "I like the classic cartoons."

"Me, too." A dimple teased the crooked side of his grin. "But if I were that cat, I'd forget that pesky mouse and go for the girl."

Dare she glance down again? No. She didn't need to. Her cotton pj's felt like fire against her bare skin, igniting each pebbled nipple. Windy swallowed, trying to moisten her dry mouth. "Now who's flirting, Sky?"

"Me," he answered softly. "The guy who has mind sex every time he looks at you."

Mind sex. She assumed he meant it just as it sounded—a celibate man's forbidden fantasies. She swallowed again, but her dry mouth refused to cooperate. Every ounce of saliva had vanished. Now she wanted his wet tongue inside her parched mouth.

Nervousness washed over her. Being aroused in cartoon-inspired pj's felt odd. Since she wanted to cover her breasts with her hair, she considered releasing the plaits in the single braid she wore, then reconsidered. The camouflage technique would probably call even more attention to her distended nipples.

She glanced at the clock. "It's late. I should go."

"No," he said quickly, his voice sounding anxious. "Stay with me. Just for a while. Neither one of us has to work tomorrow."

"I shouldn't be in your room like this."

He cocked his head. "Like what?"

Aroused. Dressed for bed and wanting to kiss you again.

"I think it would be better if we spent some time together tomorrow instead." She couldn't ignore his half-naked body, the masculine scent of his room, the sensual fluttering in her tummy. Tonight she needed to get away from the confusion of wanting him. "Good night, Sky. I'll see you in the morning."

Sky frowned as he watched her move toward the door. "You're leaving because of what I said, aren't you? That crack about the mind sex."

She stopped, turned. "It did make me uncomfortable. It's not the sort of thing we should be talking about. Especially in your bedroom at this hour."

"I'm sorry." He tugged his hand through his hair, wishing she would stay. "It was just my way of flirting. We both know nothing's going to happen. Hell, we've already slept in the same bed together." And kissed, his mind warned.

She crossed her arms, pressed them to her breasts. "We can't do that again."

"Yeah, I know." After tousling his own hair, he studied Windy's, intrigued by the loose strands that had escaped her braid. He wanted to undo that thick braid, press his face against her neck, inhale her skin. Tell her the worst of his foster care memories.

"Okay, well…" She stood in the same self-conscious manner, folded arms hiding her erect nipples. "I guess I better go."

Sky lifted his gaze and cursed the weakness running through his veins, the need to spill the emotions twisting his gut. "I can't sleep, Windy. That's why I was talking to that damn teddy bear. And that's why I want you to stay." He gripped the bed. "I don't want to be alone right now."

Her features softened. "Oh, Sky. What's wrong?"

"Lucy, I guess. Not her exactly, but what she reminds me of."

She inched forward. "Your past?"

"Yeah." Of what being unwanted and unloved had done to him. Only, unlike Lucy, he hadn't become a victim. He had victimized others instead. "I hate remembering only bits and pieces. It confuses me."

She sat beside him once again. "I'd be glad to try and help you put the pieces together."

"It's not that easy. There just isn't enough information." Liar. You remember your son. But not the child's mother. Damn it. Why couldn't he remember the boy's mother? "What the cops said about me is true. I did run away."

Why, he wondered, were his memories drifting back now? Was it because of Windy? Had she tapped into his emotions somehow? Made him think and feel, remember who and what he was?

He took a deep breath. "I know why I ran away, too."

Windy leaned forward, her soft brown eyes intent. "You do?"

"I wasn't getting along in foster care so they threatened to put me in one of those correctional institutions." A horrible feeling tightened his gut—a fear of being trapped behind concrete walls. "I took off before they could lock me up."

She touched his hand and her compassion spread through him like an undeserving balm. "Do you realize how much you've been remembering? It won't be long, Sky, before it all comes back."

Still focused on his teenage years, he looked into her eyes, wanting her to know what kind of person he had been. And God forbid, maybe deep down still was. "I even remember why they wanted to lock me up. They called me incorrigible. Said I got into too many fights, skipped too much school, drank too much beer, messed around with too many girls."

She kept her hand on his. "Foster children are often shuffled around a lot. It isn't an easy existence. You wouldn't be the first one who had rebelled."

"Don't make excuses for me," he said, as an image of his son came to mind: a black-haired boy with gray eyes so clear they could pass for silver. He figured being locked up wasn't a good enough reason to split, not when it meant leaving that beautiful child behind. He could still hear his apology to the boy. *I'm sorry. I know I said I'd always take care of you, but I can't. I ain't old enough. I don't know how.*

Not old enough. What a crock. If he was old enough to father a child, then he was sure as hell old enough to take responsibility. No excuses. If he hadn't been such a delinquent, they wouldn't have threatened to lock him up.

Windy reached up and smoothed his hair in what seemed like a maternal gesture. It made him want to snuggle against her breasts and take comfort in the feminine softness.

"When you remember something, does it happen in images or feelings?" she asked.

"Both." He watched her draw her hand back, place it on her lap. "Some things are just feelings, other things are images, like seeing myself in a dream. None of it's clear, though." He glanced at her hand again, at the slim, delicate fingers. "Like with the foster care stuff, I don't remember where I lived, but I know why I ran away. It's weird that I can remember what people said to me, but can't recall their names or faces."

"It will take time for your mind to fill in all the gaps."

"Yeah. That's what amnesia is. A gap in someone's memory."

Windy nodded and drew her legs up, tucking them beneath her. She looked cute on the corner of his bed, wearing her cartoon pajamas. The top seemed almost too big, but the shorts were just right. They rode well above her knees, exposing nicely shaped thighs. She had a small body with small curves. Her breasts weren't small, though. She had roundness there, a swell of cleavage even the baggy shirt couldn't hide. He figured men admired her class, the ladylike qualities she possessed. Not to mention the tame, girl-next-door face framed by all that wild hair. The sweet face made him smile, but the Lady Godiva mane made him hungry. Even braided or knotted into a bun, it tempted him with its sexy rebellion.

"Suddenly we're at a loss for words," she said.

"Yeah." They had been looking at each other, consumed by the intimacy of the moment, by the closeness they had just shared. Sky had never told another living soul the things he'd admitted to her. Of course, he hadn't told her all of it. Someday, though, he probably would. And when he did, she wouldn't want to hold his hand or comfort him ever again. She'd be glad to see him go.

Sky changed his thought pattern, not wanting her to see the pain creeping into his heart. "Did I tell you Melissa is coming over next Friday?"

"Charlie's daughter?"

"Yeah."

She smiled. "Tell me about her."

"Okay." He glanced at the clock, grateful for Windy's temporary company. By the end of the summer, he'd be alone again. Alone and drifting, as usual. There was no place in his life for a woman like Windy. No place at all.

Eight

"**H**i." The young girl walked into the house, then stopped to introduce herself in a friendly voice. "I'm Melissa. Sky said I didn't have to knock. He's right outside."

"I'm Windy, Sky's roommate. He told me you were visiting this evening."

"He's checking the oil in his truck," Melissa offered, rolling her brown eyes heavenward. "That old thing drinks the stuff."

Windy laughed slightly. Melissa called the vehicle old, whereas Sky referred to his '59 Apache as vintage. "Men love to tinker with old cars and trucks."

"I know." When Melissa smiled, her fine, chiseled features showed promise of a lovely young lady emerging. Sky had described the petite brunette as twelve going on thirty.

"Would you like a soda?" Windy asked, inviting the young girl into the kitchen.

"Sure. Okay." Melissa placed her backpack on the table.

"Sky's going to get pizza tonight. Are you going to eat with us?"

"Absolutely." She wouldn't miss the opportunity to spend an evening with a delightful young girl and a captivating man. Besides, the curious side of her wanted to observe Sky with Melissa. She couldn't help but watch everything he did. Psychologically, he fascinated her. He could brood one minute and laugh the next. Although he had talked about his past, she still sensed discomfort. Too often he stared into space, lost in troubled thoughts. He still needed emotional support, of that much she was sure.

As if on cue, a pair of black boots clipped across the tiled floor.

"Finally," Melissa said, drawing Windy's attention to the man entering the kitchen.

Immediately the sight of him stole her senses, the long-legged swagger making her feel like a lovesick schoolgirl. His eyes sought hers. A quick wink. A sudden smile. So fleeting was the flirtation, Windy wasn't certain if it had actually happened.

"So I see you met Missy." He smiled again, this time with his eyes.

"Yes," was all she could manage to say.

"Windy's having dinner with us," the twelve-year-old said, regarding Sky and Windy with an astute gaze.

Sky's azure eyes roamed over Windy's sundress, down her bare legs and back up. "Are you, now?"

"Yes, Skyler, I am," she responded. "I happen to adore pizza." *And you,* she added mentally, meeting his amused gaze. They were flirting, making silly conversation just for the sake of seeing each other smile. They'd been flirting all week, she realized, telling themselves it was harmless. They were friends—a man who had chosen celibacy and a woman still protecting her virginity. A summer fling wasn't possible.

"Go get the pizza, Sky," Melissa said, practically pushing him out the door. "I'm hungry."

"Do you girls wanna ride along?" he asked.

"Nope." She glanced back at Windy. "We'll both stay here."

As he shrugged and turned to leave, Windy suggested adding a salad to their meal, and Melissa readily agreed. Within minutes the girls were alone in the gingham kitchen getting acquainted while Sky zoomed out of the driveway.

Melissa cut into one of Windy's homegrown tomatoes. She kept potted vegetables on the patio and herbs on the windowsill. Nothing, though, could compare to the avocados the ancient tree produced. Several awaited their turn to be sliced.

"Windy, do you like to cook?"

"Love it, do you?"

"Yeah, I help my mom all the time." Melissa scooped the juicy tomato wedges into a bowl. "Do you want to get married someday?"

An answer formed quickly, naturally. "Absolutely. I've been planning my wedding for years." Traditional elegance, she thought: a silk gown with Irish lace and a sea of pearls, roses and tall white candles, a professional photographer, bridesmaids, ushers in tuxedos. "All I need is the groom."

"What about Sky?"

Windy set the lettuce aside, concerned about where Melissa intended to take this girl-talk conversation. She answered the safest way she knew how. "What about him?"

"He likes you."

"Of course he does. We're friends." But even as she said it, her heart nearly beat its way out of her chest. She knew what the phrase *He likes you* meant in junior-high terms. And Melissa, in all her maturity, was still a twelve-year-old who spoke that adolescent language.

The persistent young girl pushed a little further. "My mom thinks he wants to be more than your friend. She says you're the first girl he's ever talked about."

Oh, no. Matchmaking for her and Sky. "I'm the first girl he's ever lived with." Anxious to turn the tables, she tilted her head and grinned at Melissa. "Speaking of boys, is there one at school you like?"

"Nicky Cardinal." The name came out in one long, dramatic sigh. "He's Italian."

Windy smiled. "Does Nicky know you like him?"

Melissa studied an avocado, then grinned. "Uh-huh. My girlfriend told him. And he's been really nice to me ever since."

"Do you ride your bike by his house on weekends?"

The young girl giggled. "No. I walk. And I wear my cutest outfits. He's older than me."

Maternal protection kicked in. "How much older?"

"A year. He's in eighth grade."

They continued to talk while they prepared the salad, slicing and dicing, then adding grated cheddar cheese and croutons on top. Windy learned about Nicky Cardinal's wavy brown hair and skateboarding skills, along with his recent chipped tooth and interest in archeology. Twenty minutes later, when they had exhausted that male topic, Melissa went right back to their original subject—the tall, blue-eyed one.

"Windy, if Sky asked you, would you go out with him?"

"You mean…like on a date?"

"Yeah."

"We're just friends. He would never ask me out."

The young girl persisted. "Just say he did, hypothetically."

Windy glanced up at the ceiling, nibbled her bottom lip. Date Sky? Oh, why not? She hadn't dated anyone in quite a while, and the man did fascinate her. Besides, hypothetically, a friendly date wouldn't change the course of their lives. He'd still be gone by the end of the summer. "Sure, I'd go out with him."

Melissa grinned. "Would you kiss him?"

Immediately a stream of heat pooled low in her belly. She couldn't tell Melissa the truth, that she'd already indulged in that fantasy. "What woman wouldn't want to kiss Sky?" she said, hoping her response sounded generic.

The girl proceeded to set the table, grinning when the front door opened. "He's back."

Sky entered the kitchen, pizza boxes in hand. "Hey, ladies."

Windy found herself staring. How many times had she re-lived that kiss in her mind? Recalled the feel of Sky's hands on her skin, the texture of his beard stubble, the flavor of his lips?

He placed the food on the counter. "Pepperoni for me and Missy, and vegetarian for you, Windy. I'd say we're ready to eat."

Windy peered into the box deemed hers. "How did you know I was a vegetarian?" She had been prepared to pick the pepperoni off. She didn't like to burden people with her se-lective food choices.

"Hell, we live together. I've been noticing all kinds of things about you."

Windy observed him through a curious gaze. Simple as his statement was, it struck her as personal. Almost intimate. And it made her realize the strength of their attraction. Apparently he had been watching her the way she watched him, studying her every move, her habits, likes and dislikes. She moistened her lips. Now she wanted to kiss him again even more.

As they shared the meal, Sky smiled. He knew Melissa and Windy would hit if off. They already seemed like old friends, but then females were like that—secretive and girlish, no mat-ter what their age. And females liked rabbit food, he decided, as Windy poured dressing over her salad. Few men would fill up on greens when they could eat pizza.

Melissa sipped her soda, then wiped her mouth, looking ladylike beyond her years. "Do you know what my mom thinks, Sky?"

"What?" he asked, helping himself to another pizza slice.

"That you and Windy should go on a date."

Windy gasped, and he dropped the pizza, cheese side down, onto his plate. How was he supposed to respond? Especially with his heartbeat skittering. He'd already tried that date rou-tine with Windy. Sort of. Offering to teach her to ride had been his way of asking her out. And she'd refused. Just as well, he figured, since they had agreed not to get romantically involved.

He stole a quick glance at Windy. Lord, he felt like a fool.

"Melissa's friend told Nicky Cardinal that Melissa likes him," Windy said, breaking through the awkward silence in a shaky sort of voice.

He had no idea who Nicky Cardinal was, but he assumed the information was relevant. Somehow.

"That's right," Missy chimed. "And now Nicky's really nice to me."

"Oh, I see." Apparently Melissa had decided he liked Windy and thought it was her feminine duty to prod him into being nice to her. "Well, I'm glad Nicky likes you." Okay, got through that one, he told himself, now change the subject. "Good pizza, huh?"

Melissa glanced at the gooey mess on his plate. "So are you going to ask Windy out or not? You know, she just might surprise you and say yes."

Windy's face flushed, and Sky felt a smile pull at his lips. So, the girls did have a secret. And clearly he was part of it. Suddenly he felt like a kid, green as hell, his knees nearly knocking.

To hell with not getting romantically involved. "So do you want to?" he asked.

She nodded somewhat shyly. "Sure."

He tried to look more relaxed than he felt. What he used to do wasn't really dating, not in the proper sense of the word. Hell, maybe this was going to be his first real date. "How about tomorrow at six?"

"Sure, but I have a hair appointment at five-thirty. I probably won't be ready until closer to seven."

"That's fine. I can drop you off at the salon, then pick you up afterward. We can go out from there." He leaned forward. "You're not getting your hair cut, are you?"

"No. My hairdresser convinced me to have a few pieces highlighted." She lifted a strand of her hair. "Just in front."

"As long as you don't cut it." He wanted to tangle his hands in that sexy mane, wrap his fingers around those rebellious curls.

Melissa clanked her fork against her salad bowl. "People kiss on dates, you know," she said, a pleased-as-pie expression on her face.

"Yeah, I know." Sky balled up a napkin and tossed it at the twelve-year-old before he died of embarrassment. He had no intention of talking about kissing in front of Melissa.

She flung the paper ball back, hitting him square in the forehead. They looked at each other, then burst into short peals of laugher. Windy smiled from across the table, and Sky's heart dove right for his throat. Pretty Windy. Lord, but he wanted her in the worst way.

Reminding herself to breathe, Windy checked her appearance once again in one of the many mirrors in the beauty salon. If Sky didn't show up soon, she was going to have a full-blown panic attack. Maybe this date wasn't such a good idea, after all.

"Your hair came out great." The flamboyant stylist lifted a can of diet soda to her burgundy lips, then twined a strand of her own red locks. "Perfect, in fact."

"Thanks." Okay, so her hair looked good, but what about her dress? Windy tugged on the bodice. Oh, for Pete's sake. What had possessed her to buy black lycra? She didn't look like a teacher. She looked like a hussy. Dang it. She should have brought something else to wear, something more conservative.

"Too much cleavage?" She whirled around to face the other woman.

"If you've got it, flaunt it." The stylist gave Windy's hair one last fluff. "Stop worrying, you look hot."

Too much cleavage. Flaunting wasn't Windy's style. One last yank brought the neckline up to an almost respectable level.

"Talk about hot!" The other woman let out a low whistle.

"That gorgeous guy who just walked in the door wouldn't happen to be your date, would he?"

Windy peered around the redhead's voluptuous figure. "My date and my new roommate."

"You live with him? Lucky girl."

"Yes, I am," Windy said, uncomfortably aware that every female stylist in the salon was gawking at Sky. Possibly some of the male stylists, too.

Windy smiled as she approached him. Trust Sky to hide behind a pair of sunglasses and a Stetson. He wasn't about to walk into a building full of strangers and reveal a thing.

The Western attire he wore looked new. White piping lined the collar, cuffs and pockets of a long-sleeved black shirt. A sterling silver concho belt, black jeans and shiny boots completed the tall, dark and handsome package. Somehow, Windy thought, Sky's clean natural virility made the hi-tech atmosphere of the salon appear gaudy.

"Damn," he said when she stood before him.

"Damn?" Confused, she questioned the curse. She preferred to look someone in the eye when conversing with them. He was cheating behind the sunglasses.

"Damn, you look good." He grinned—a slightly boyish, slightly flirtatious smile she recognized all too well.

He took her hand, and they walked out to the parking lot, both silent. When they reached his truck and Sky opened the door for her, Windy halted. A long-stemmed, single red rose graced the bench seat.

She melted, then lifted the flower and inhaled its romantic scent. Red roses meant passion. Would he know that?

"I thought we'd head south a little," he said, steering the truck toward the freeway entrance. "To the beach. There's a restaurant near the pier I like. That okay?"

Tongue-tied and nervous, she nodded.

Sky reached for a CD. "Country okay?"

Again, she nodded.

He placed the CD in the player. "You're awful quiet," he noted when the music started.

Windy listened to the familiar lyrics of the first song. "I'm nervous."

"Really?" He sounded surprised. "About going out with me? Hell, honey, we live together. Just think of us as two friends having dinner."

She sent him a shaky smile. The suggestion was impossible, especially since she kept wondering if their evening would end with a good-night kiss.

Almost an hour later, when they arrived at the restaurant, she took a deep, cleansing breath. The Italian bistro, located a block from the ocean and housed in an ornate Victorian-style building, supplied valet parking, but didn't take reservations. Sky said he preferred it that way. Unlike Windy, he wasn't one to live by the clock.

Writing down the name Skyler, the hostess informed them of the twenty-minute wait. They decided to spend that time in the bar.

Without thinking, Windy reached up and removed Sky's sunglasses. Too often he neglected them when entering a building.

In turn, he lifted his hand to graze her cheek. "You want a glass of wine or something?" He traced the angles of her face. "It will take the edge off, honey."

Windy had yet to relax, but now she felt downright mushy. And a little dizzy. "Okay."

"You look so pretty." He rubbed his index finger back and forth over the clear gloss she wore on her lips, as though waiting for a smile.

He didn't wait long. Every inch of her smiled and warmed at his touch.

The cocktail waitress interrupted the intimate moment. Windy ordered a glass of zinfandel and Sky decided on a soft drink.

"It's honey-flavored," Windy said, watching him press his fingers together. "The lip gloss," she explained when he gave her a puzzled look.

Now it was his turn to smile. "Will I get to taste it?"

She nodded as her heart skipped a beat. Tasting her lip gloss meant kissing her, didn't it?

Their dinner conversation flowed fairly easily, even though that impending kiss still occupied a portion of Windy's mind. She adjusted the napkin on her lap, then dipped into a plate of manicotti. "This is good."

"Yeah, mine, too." Sky twirled spaghetti around his fork. "Hey, have you thought any more about going riding with me?"

She couldn't help but smile. "Are you asking me on another date already?"

He grinned back at her. "Yeah, I guess I am."

How could she refuse those boyish dimples? "Then I'd love to." It was time, she decided, to face her fears and forget about that childhood fall. Besides, Sky had made trail riding sound glorious—a trip to Heaven.

When they sat silent for a moment, she initiated another conversation, a neutral one she hoped. A trip to Heaven had her thinking about that kiss again. "Did I tell you my father was a musician?" she asked.

"No, you haven't mentioned your family at all."

Family. The word set off a loud alarm in her head. Some neutral subject. Sky didn't have a family, yet here she was, ready to babble about hers.

Sky shook his head. "Hey, none of that. Don't think you can't mention your family around me. I can handle it." He lifted his fork and skewered a meatball. "Now tell me about your musician father."

Grateful for his casual manner, she relaxed a little. "I don't remember him well. He died when I was four. Originally my parents were from Ohio. They moved to California so my dad could pursue his career. He had hoped to find work as a studio musician." She buttered a slice of warm bread, recalling what she'd been told about her father. "He never did, though. He worked as a guitar instructor at a music store instead."

"What about your mom? What did she do?"

"She was an elementary schoolteacher, just like Edith. I really miss her."

"Edith told me she died a few years ago."

"She was a good mom." Windy pictured her mother's sunny smile and casual manner. "It's never easy raising a child alone, but she did her best."

Sky twirled another bite of spaghetti around his fork, but didn't bring it to his lips. "You'll be a good mom, too."

"Thank you. When the time comes, I'll certainly do my best." She tasted the bread, thinking his words sweeter than the melted butter. "Being a parent is the most important job in the world. I mean, think about it. You're responsible for another human being. It goes beyond nine-to-five, and there are no weekends off or early retirement. Once you have a child, you'll always be a parent."

The change in his expression resulted in a furrowed brow. "That proves some people shouldn't have kids."

"I'd have to agree with you there." She wanted to reach across the table and slip her hand in his, touch him, feel his pulse. "But you're not one of those people, Sky. You'll make a terrific father someday."

His breath expanded. "You've got it wrong, Pretty Windy. That whole thing scares the hell out of me."

Because of his upbringing, she thought. Because he hadn't grown up in a healthy, nurturing environment. Now she understood that the loneliness of his childhood had brought about those disturbing frowns. He didn't really have an aversion to kids. "You were wonderful with Melissa last night. She absolutely adores you."

"I've known her all her life. That's different."

Windy smiled. "And if you had a child, don't you think you'd know that child all its life? It's the same thing, only better." She wagged her fork at him. "Nothing you say will make me change my mind. You've got it in you to be a dad."

He glanced down at his plate. "Do you think I'd be all right with a teenager? I hear they're pretty tough to handle."

Although she thought the question odd, she answered it casually. "Melissa is almost a teenager."

"But she's a girl."

Apparently he assumed boys were harder to raise. Another conclusion drawn from his own experiences, she thought. After all, he had been an incorrigible youth. "It's not as if a teenage boy is going to drop into your life. If you have a son, you'll raise him from infancy. And you'll do just fine."

He looked up, breathed heavily, glanced back down, breathed audibly again, then pushed his plate away.

"Sky? What's the matter?"

"Huh?" His gaze caught hers. "Nothin'. It's just you have the wrong impression of me."

"No. You have the wrong impression of you."

His voice turned hard. "No. You do. I don't wanna get married and I'm not the dad type. Responsibility isn't my style." He narrowed his eyes into protective slits. "What you see is what you want to see. It's not what's really there. Good and decent I'm not."

The arrow that pierced Windy's heart reached her soul in one sharp jab. What he'd said frightened the woman in her. Not the friend or the future psychologist, but the woman. She fought a wave of panic. Sensible Windy had taken an unexpected turn and fallen head over dangerous heels for the wrong man.

Wrong? No, he wasn't wrong. He was troubled. And he needed her unwavering support. She smiled a shaky smile. "I already told you, nothing you say will change my mind about you. You're one of the good guys, Sky."

His lips broke into a grin. "And you, Pretty Windy, are stubborn as hell."

She sipped her water. "Truthfully, I'm still a bit nervous." Especially since that romantic night in bed had come whirling back into her mind. Which, she decided, accounted for her disjointed emotions, her sudden urge to undress him, kiss and touch and make him as weak-kneed as she.

"Really? You seem fine."

"Do I?"

He continued to grin. "Yeah. Ladylike and proper."

He looked sexy, his hair dipping over his forehead, his cheekbones shadowed by the flickering candlelight. And those dimples, those boyish, rakish dimples. She had never wanted to touch a man so badly in her life.

Windy slid her fingers down the cool exterior of her water glass, her voice sultry, even to her own ears. "Sometimes I have improper thoughts." Unconsciously she moistened her lips. "Wild thoughts." Like the ones scrambling around in her head at this very moment. "Lately I've been fantasizing about us," she whispered, as a flare of heat surged through her veins.

At first Sky only stared, then shifted uncomfortably in his seat as though his jeans had suddenly grown too tight. "Me, too," he said finally, the hunger in his eyes barely contained.

"Oh…" Windy became flustered, realizing how blatantly sexual her admission had been. "I shouldn't have said that." Thoroughly embarrassed, she pushed her glass away. "I'm sorry."

He shifted again. "Hey, there's no need to apologize. We're both young, healthy adults living in the same house. Hell, we're bound to—"

As luck would have it, the busboy chose that moment to refill their glasses, stilling Sky's next words. After the boy moved on, Sky lifted his water and took a huge swallow, looking as though he wanted to douse himself with it instead— cool his raging hormones. "What do you say…should we go for a walk? Maybe check out the pier?"

Windy nodded, grateful for the suggestion. What she needed right now was air—plenty of brisk, clean air.

Nine

A warm summer breeze, salty sea air and a bright moon welcomed them. Hands clasped, Sky and Windy walked silently to the pier.

They stood on the boardwalk and leaned against the rail, mesmerized by the dark ocean below. Flowing and foaming, the water swayed into gentle, mystical waves.

As powerful as the ocean's current was the need Sky felt for this woman. A need that went beyond lust. A need so strong it terrified him.

He turned toward Windy, admiring her in the moonlight. The wind lifted her long hair, whipping it freely. He caught a golden strand, then held his breath. Oh, dear God, how he craved her.

Windy closed her eyes and shivered, her flesh clearly tingling with a craving of its own. "Are you cold?" he asked, a loose tendril of her hair still within his grasp.

She opened her eyes and slowly, very slowly, shook her head. "I'm nervous again."

Sky removed his hat and stepped closer. "Sweet Pretty Windy," he said, pressing his forehead to hers. "You're so innocent."

She swallowed. "I suppose I am, compared to the women you're probably used to."

"Yeah." He lowered his chin and brazenly stared down at the cleavage her dress revealed. She might be innocent, but she looked like a vixen tonight. A sultry goddess.

"Sky, what are you doing?"

"Looking down your dress. I like it."

She scolded him in a soft voice. "That's not a very polite thing to do."

"Sorry." He lifted his head. "I've been thinking about doing that all night. Couldn't help myself."

Windy laughed, the throaty sound honest and free. "You're wicked, you know that?"

Wicked? Quickly he bent his head to nuzzle her cleavage. He'd show her wicked.

"Oh, my goodness...now what are you doing?" She squirmed and giggled. When his hair fell across the top of her breasts, she delved into it.

An elderly couple walked by. The man peered over his shoulder as the woman snorted. Clearly embarrassed, Windy giggled again. "Sky, we're making a spectacle of ourselves."

"We are?" He brought his face up next to hers. "Then let's go play on the beach."

"I'm not dressed to play on the beach."

He rubbed his forehead hypnotically across hers. "Then let me undress you so we can go play on the beach."

"You're teasing me." She buried her hands in his hair and let the silkiness spill out over her wrists and down her arms.

"I think about undressing you. I think about it all the time."

A soft moan escaped her lips. "You undress me with your eyes. You make me feel vulnerable."

Sky smoothed his cheek against hers. "I don't want to make you feel vulnerable, Windy," he whispered. "I want to make you feel good.'' He moved closer, daring her to feel his raging arousal.

As her body swayed, she gripped his arms for support and breathed deeply. "Do you want to taste my lip gloss now?" she asked, her voice soft and tempting.

She looked as creamy and sweet as a hot-fudge sundae, her caramel eyes warm and glazed.

Accepting what was offered, he leaned in and flicked his tongue across her lips, tasting the sweet essence of a woman and the honeyed cosmetic she wore.

Like a feral beast, Windy's passion clawed back at him. Cupping his face, she tasted him. Frantically her tongue laved over his lips and down his chin until she latched on to his neck and nipped the pulsing flesh.

Sky nearly erupted on the spot.

Since he still held his hat in one hand, he dropped the Stetson to the ground and used both hands to pull her face up to his. They kissed. Ferociously uncontrolled, the moist contact was openmouthed and carnal. When his tongue thrust into her mouth, she met it desperately. Over and over they kissed, stopping sporadically for small breaths of salty air.

Windy's hands found the back pockets on his jeans. Slipping inside each one, she urged his hips toward her and then arched and rubbed against him like a feline pleading to be stroked. Sensing her need, he complied, caressing every part of her within his reach.

She felt good. So damn good. The thrust of her tongue made him want to carry her to the beach and lay her in the sand. Bury himself so deep within her their bodies would move as one. Stroke her until she purred and climaxed beneath him.

Caught up in his fantasy, Sky began to lift her off the ground. His mind was filled with sex—carnal images and primal urges. He intended to cradle her rear, wrap her legs around his waist and rub his heat against hers. He didn't care if they were standing in a public place, going after each other like a couple of oversexed alley cats.

But apparently she did. Quickly she shoved him away, breaking the contact.

"What's wrong?" he asked, although he knew.

Windy only stared back at him, openmouthed.

Tempted to push his tongue back into that open mouth, his gaze raked across the woman feeding his desire.

"Sky," Windy said his name as if there were an explanation in it. Widening her eyes, she laughed a little. A shy, embarrassed laugh.

He looked around. A few people were strolling up and down the pier, some were seated on nearby benches, sipping gourmet coffee. One tattered old man was fishing. No one seemed to be paying any attention to them, at least not now.

"Do you think we had an audience?" he asked, suddenly craving a smoke. Sky damned himself for quitting. He still had an urge to keep his mouth busy.

Windy shrugged, still visibly embarrassed. "We were…I mean, we shouldn't have been…"

"We were kissing, honey." He flashed a grin rife with mischief. "And it felt good. *Damn* good. Best mind sex I've ever had."

"Sky!"

"Admit it," he said, teasing her. "You were having mind sex, too."

She blushed. "You're wicked, Skyler."

He laughed. "Admit it, Pretty Windy. You were thinking about—"

"Okay," she interrupted quickly, a rosy hue still staining her cheeks. "I was. But we were getting carried away. I've never acted like that in public before."

Sky fumbled with the cigarettes in his shirt pocket as a small breeze tousled his hair. "Told ya we should have played on the beach. It's quieter down there."

"We probably would have been arrested," Windy muttered, as she tugged on her dress self-consciously.

He laughed. "Can you imagine what Edith would have done when we called her to bail us out of jail?"

"She would have skinned you alive." Windy smiled and stepped into his arms, where he wished she could stay.

"Do you want to get some dessert?" he asked, hugging her.

"Sure." She looked up at him. "Where's your hat?"

"Oh, hell."

They separated and searched the immediate ground. The hat was nowhere to be seen, but he wasn't about to go combing the length of the pier. Scouting around in the dark looking for a black hat wasn't his idea of fun. Chalk it up to experience. He could always buy another hat. Freeing his hands to touch Windy was worth the two hundred bucks. She had to be the wildest little creature he had ever kissed. Pretty Windy's passion was as untamed as her windblown hair.

"Do you think somebody stole your hat?"

"Maybe." Sky looked down at the crashing waves below. "Or it blew overboard."

"Did you drop it?"

"Yeah, on purpose," he answered with a dastardly grin. "The damn thing was in the way."

She chuckled. "You're adorable, Sky."

"Puppies are adorable," he said, suddenly bothered by her affection. "Guys like me are dangerous."

He had no right to want her so badly or to lure her into wanting him. She was right. They had gone too far. Tonight, he decided, would be their first and last date, otherwise he'd end up taking complete advantage of her. He'd done enough rotten things in his life and had no intention of hurting Windy. She deserved better. This date was a mistake and so was that mind-blowing kiss.

"Let's go get that dessert," he said. They needed to talk.

Seated side by side on a wrought-iron bench in front of the ice cream parlor, they ate dessert. While Windy lapped one scoop of fat-free chocolate yogurt, Sky worked heartily on a doubled-decker French vanilla ice cream cone.

As his tongue slid over the ice cream, she admonished herself. Watching a man eat shouldn't make her feel weak-kneed, yet every time Sky lifted food to his mouth, her body surged with a hunger of its own—a need she had never experienced before. She had kissed other men, but none of the clean-cut professionals she'd dated had ever made her fantasize about losing her virginity. But Sky, gorgeous, wild-spirited Sky, had ignited a sensual fire in every cell of her being.

They finished their dessert in silence, both, she realized, lost in their own thoughts. At times she wished she could read his mind. The man was as unpredictable as a summer rain. Much too often his easy manner and boyish smile faltered. Like now, she thought, noticing the furrow in his brow and clouds darkening his eyes. They sat beneath the incandescent glow of a streetlight. She could see his expression vividly, and it reflected a mood change.

He deposited their soiled napkins in a nearby trash can and resumed his seat, his legs spread, his hands idle against his knees. The loose posture was his signature, a part of his defy-the-rules nature. And it was, unfortunately, one of the habits that made him appealing—so different from the kind of man with whom Windy envisioned herself falling in love.

Love? She stared at the road as a car full of teenagers breezed by. What had made her think that? Her hormones, she told herself, combined with the equally stimulating effects of salty air and a hair-tousling breeze. Yeah, right. What about the cowboy who dominated her thoughts, the blue-eyed drifter who invaded her dreams? Wasn't he responsible for her feelings? Her fear of falling in love?

Yes, she thought, turning to look at him once again. He was. Their flirtations weren't harmless. Something more than friendship brewed between them. Windy took a deep breath. She didn't believe in living in denial. If her heart had become entangled with his, then she would have to deal with that. Another time, she told herself. When they weren't sharing an enchanted beach setting, when she wasn't aching to touch him so badly. Right now she wanted to kiss his disturbing frown away.

Sky caught her eye and cleared his throat as if preparing for a speech. "Honey, there's something we need to talk about."

For a moment Windy panicked. Did he know her feelings went beyond lust? That she battled with her emotions? Or that suddenly she wanted to keep him forever?

"I don't think we should go on another date," he said. "Or kiss each other again."

The heart entangled with his began to hurt. "Why not?"

He braced his back against the bench, but kept his eyes on hers. "Because this celibacy thing isn't easy, and kissing you makes me want to give it up." He pulled a hand through his hair. "And you're not like the other women I've dated. You don't just fall into bed with every cowboy who comes your way. You're saving yourself for the right guy."

And you might be him, she wanted to say. "People can date without sleeping together."

He laughed, a bit sardonically. "I can't. And besides we live together. Our rooms are a thin wall apart." Quickly his laughter faded. "If we made love, you'd only end up getting hurt. Dating isn't worth the risk."

Windy bristled. "My virginity isn't a disease, Sky. It's a choice. The way your celibacy is. And we're both capable of spending time together without making love." She wanted to date him, explore his texture, his masculine scent, his exotic flavor. And she wanted him to wonder if he was falling in love with her—to think of her as more than a forbidden sexual partner. "Sex doesn't have to be a part of dating or getting to know someone. Maybe it's time you learned how to have a relationship with a woman without taking her to bed first."

"Oh, this is just great." Clearly agitated, he tossed his hands in the air. "Now you're turning this into one of your psychology lessons."

She crossed her arms. "I am not."

"Yes, you are. And it's a dangerous lesson, Windy. Because you want to pretend this is the fifties or something, and we can hold hands and neck at the front door without going any further." His cloudy gaze bore into hers. "I'm not built that way. And I'm too damn attracted to you to put myself through that kind of agony. It's all or nothing with me, honey."

Windy closed her eyes, gulped some air, then opened them. She had never been so confused in her life. Here she was encouraging Sky to get involved with her, when deep down she knew he wasn't the man with whom she should want to share a life.

"I don't want to talk about this tonight," she said. "I just can't think clearly."

He tapped a finger to her chin. "Well, think about this. Regardless of what you say, if we started touching each other all the time, we'd end up in bed. And believe me, next time I'd do a lot more than kiss you." He moved his finger to her lips, traced them longingly, then pulled back. "And you're the type of girl who would want a commitment from the man she's sleeping with. And I'm not the sort of guy who could give you anything more than good and tender sex."

Windy swallowed. Good and tender sex sounded almost romantic coming from him. But to an extent, he was right. If they continued to date, they probably would end up in bed together. She wouldn't allow it to happen out of sheer lust, though. She would only sleep with a man she loved. And loving him was possible. Her heart had already made that deduction.

"So we're back to being roommates," she said. And she was back to helping a troubled man and setting him free.

Sky nodded. "Yeah."

I'll fight falling in love with him, she decided. I'll be his friend, but I won't allow myself to ache for him, or dream about him at night. Windy straightened her spine. She would find the right man someday—one who wanted to get married and raise a houseful of children.

He gazed out at the highway. "I guess we should head home," he said, although he didn't stand to leave.

She managed a heavyhearted smile when he finally turned

her way and removed the truck key from his pocket. "I had a nice time, Sky. Thank you."

"Sure."

As they walked back to the restaurant where his truck was parked, they didn't hold hands. And she knew they wouldn't kiss good-night, either. Their brief romantic interlude had ended.

Two weekends later Windy and Sky agreed to keep their horseback riding "date," although now they referred to it as a friendly outing rather than a romantic one.

Sky had hitched up a trailer and loaded a sturdy brown-and-white paint, which stood patiently while Sky taught Windy some basic horse rules. He didn't bombard her with too much information, for which she was grateful. He seemed more concerned about her just relaxing and enjoying herself.

"He's so big." She stroked the gelding's nose apprehensively. Her fear of horses had stemmed from a childhood fall, and although she hadn't been injured, she remembered the tumble had seemed like a long way down. She preferred animals who were low to the ground. Not as low as snakes, though. Something in between. Like dogs.

"Big doesn't mean dangerous, you know," Sky drawled, looking amused, his blue eyes sparkling beneath a new black Stetson.

Windy turned to look up at him, and the horse pawed the ground. Sky gave the gelding a light nudge with his elbow, and it eyed Windy as though she had corrected it. "He wants you to pet him again," he said, grinning a little devilishly. "Us big guys like to be touched."

Windy narrowed her eyes. Oh, for Pete's sake. "So now you're flirting, Sky? Two weeks ago you lectured me on how we shouldn't touch each other. It would be nice if you'd make up your mind."

"Sorry." He winced sheepishly. "If I don't flirt, I don't know how else to talk to a woman. And just because I said what I did doesn't mean I'm not going to get turned on being around you. Pretending we're not attracted to each other is kind of stupid, don't you think? At least if we drool over each other, it's honest.''

"I suppose." Heat rose to her cheeks. As she brought her hand back up to pet the paint, Sky studied her fingers. Now she felt self-conscious. She was wearing freshly washed blue jeans, lizard-skin boots and a top tied at her waist. Judging from the hungry way in which Sky was eyeing her, she was certain once he was seated behind her on the horse, he'd be peering down her blouse every chance he got.

The paint was tacked up and ready to go. Since she wanted to ride double, Sky had said a saddle was out of the question. Too uncomfortable. He'd claimed a bareback pad would be more appropriate, one equipped with stirrups and a handhold.

"I'll help you mount up."

Windy reached for the handhold and slipped her boot into the stirrup. Sky clamped his hands around her waist and suddenly she felt boneless and weak.

"Are you all right?" he asked. Apparently she was melting against him.

"I'm a little nervous." She was more than nervous. Man and beast were turning her limbs to mush.

"I'll be right behind you, honey, soon as I adjust your stirrups." He hoisted her up and handed her the reins.

She held the reins loosely and looked around. The trees didn't look so tall from this angle. In fact, some of the branches looked a might low, and she wondered how they were going to travel down the narrow dirt path without being scratched to death.

He explained how the stirrups should feel, asked her if she was comfortable, then pressed the heel of her boot down. She said something about having taken ballet lessons when she was a kid, and he chuckled. Automatically her toes pointed down again and she corrected them quickly. Toes up. Heels down. She thought her legs might cramp.

"Scoot forward, honey," he said, easing himself up behind her.

He felt good. Big and safe. His arms came forward and she leaned back a little. He was close. Real close. But she didn't mind.

The paint, registered as Mister Bear Robin, was simply called Robin. Windy liked him. He felt like a rocking horse that snorted once in a while to remind you he was flesh and bone. Sky kept his arms around her, instructing as they moved down the dirt path.

For the next two hours they enjoyed the richness of the land, the forbidden feel of each other. Windy guided Robin with the reins but was certain Sky gave the horse subtle commands with his legs. They stayed on the wider paths, on low ground and crossed a small body of water. Eventually they came to a shady area where they stopped to have their picnic.

He dismounted first, then helped her down. When her feet touched the earth she wobbled, and he held her, his Stetson creating a sun shield. They stood, gazing at each other, and he smiled and touched her cheek. "You did good, honey."

"Thanks." She gripped his arms, still weaving a little. "I don't think I'm ready to ride alone, though."

He winked. The boyish flirtation warmed her lovesick heart. "Give yourself time."

Sky hobbled the gelding while Windy unpacked their lunch. He joined her beneath a tall eucalyptus tree, and she handed him a brown paper bag. He opened a soft drink and ate his potato chips before unwrapping the sandwich.

Windy nibbled on a rice cake and Sky winced. "That looks kinda bland."

"It's a healthy snack," she responded, thinking how good his potato chips looked. Greasy, crunchy and fattening.

With a can of cola perched between his legs, salty chips in hand, he shrugged, then grinned. "I wouldn't know about eating healthy."

It amazed Windy that he could eat such junk yet maintain that brawny body. There wasn't an ounce of wasted flesh on Sky. He was lean and toned to perfection. Then again, he was athletic and active. A man who thrived outdoors. A blue-eyed, Native American Tarzan.

"So what are you going to do for your birthday?" he asked.

"How did you know my birthday was coming up?"

"Edith told me."

"Of course," she said, then answered his original question. "A friend is taking me out. We'll probably go to dinner, then maybe to a movie afterward."

"Oh." His eyes turned dark. "Is this friend a guy?"

She suppressed a smile. Apparently Tarzan was jealous. "A girl. Another teacher where I work."

He glanced down at his sandwich, then back up, his lips tilting crookedly. "Do you believe in astrology? You know, birth signs and all that."

Windy popped a grape into her mouth, shaking her head as she chewed. "Not really, no. Do you?"

He shrugged. "I don't know. Sometimes the personality traits seem pretty true. Like you're a Cancer. Or a Moonchild, as some people prefer to call it. Anyway, from what I've read, you fit the bill."

"Really?" The fact that he'd read about her astrological sign pleased her, even if she didn't believe in fortune telling. "So what is a Moonchild supposed to be like?"

"Family oriented. Sensitive, gentle-natured. And the women are maternal, the type who love kids."

"Gee, that does sound like me."

He flashed his dimples. "Told ya."

Her heart tripped. Dang that schoolboy smile. "So what sign are you?"

"Scorpio. At least I think I am. I'm not sure if that fake ID had my true birthday or not."

Windy appreciated that he spoke about his past fairly easily with her now, even if he frowned whenever he broached the subject. "There wouldn't have been any reason for you to change the month and day, just the year."

"Yeah, I guess. And Scorpios are supposed to be highly sexual beings so…"

"So celibacy must be really difficult for you."

"Truthfully," he said, after swallowing another gulp of soda, "I was doing okay until I met you. My undue suffering is all your fault."

"Oh, please." She jabbed his ribs and watched his silly grin widen. "I'm hardly a diva."

"Then you must have put a sex spell on me, little teacher, because jumping your bones is all I think about."

Windy pushed away a flare of anger that surfaced. She would have preferred a love spell, but hid her disappointment, trying to ignore his ungentlemanly admission. Jumping her bones didn't quite compare to her fantasy about making love. Somehow, they didn't sound as if they meant the same thing. He would never fall in love with her, she realized. All she was to him was a sexual fantasy.

Sky removed his shirt, laid it on the grass, then reached for Windy, urging her to enjoy the sunshine with him. Within moments they were side by side, their heads resting on his shirt, his hat propped upon his naked chest. She plucked another grape and offered it to him, telling herself to forget about her romantic notions. At least they were friends.

He eyed the grape curiously before sucking it into his mouth. "Did you know that if you cut a wild grapevine and spread your hair under the sap, it'll grow long and luxuriant, like the vine?"

"Who told you that?"

He tickled her cheek with a strand of his hair. "Creek beauty secret."

Windy moved a little closer. "What else do the Creeks believe?"

"Well…" Sky looked thoughtful before he responded, his lips tilting in an impish smile. "If a person doesn't spit four times when he sees a shooting star, he'll go blind or all his teeth will fall out."

She squeezed his arm playfully. "You made that up."

"I did not." He raised three fingers in a mock Boy Scout pledge. "Honest, honey."

Windy rolled her eyes and Sky laughed. "I'd rather wish upon a shooting star," she said. "Wouldn't you?"

"Yeah."

His wistful tone prompted her next question. "So what would you wish for?"

"I'd change the past, I suppose."

"How so?"

"I'd fix some of my mistakes. Do things differently."

Windy hoped he'd continue, but he chose to study the tree instead. "What things, Sky?"

"Stuff I don't want to get into right now." He glanced over at her. "I know you want to help me accept who I am and what I've done, but talking about it isn't going to change anything. I have to handle things on my own."

What things? she wanted to shout. And what had he done that had him disliking himself? "Just remember if you ever do need to talk, I'm here, okay?"

"Okay."

As Sky gazed up at the eucalyptus branches again, a hawk chose that moment to take wing and fly. The rustling leaves and magnificence of the bird startled Windy. She gasped and Sky swallowed. Neither said a word as the hawk soared away.

Ten

Sky allowed his gaze to roam over the woman standing beside the stove. She was humming a familiar tune he couldn't quite place. The lilting sound washed over him like an aphrodisiac.

She looked slightly mussed yet beautiful. A simple blue dress hugged her waist, flowing loosely to her ankles. Her feet were bare, her wild locks gathered into a loose ponytail. He studied her svelte form, then sighed. His eyes were becoming accustomed to the length and contour of her body, but his hands were sorely deprived.

Windy turned and caught him red-handed. "How long have you been standing there?"

His Adam's apple bobbed. "Not long."

She set the spoon down. She had been stirring a big pot of something that smelled really good. "Why do you do that? Sneak up on me?"

Immediately he got defensive. "I don't sneak."

Her hands flew to her hips in a womanly gesture. "Yes, you do. You do it all the time."

"Are you trying to pick a fight or something?"

"No. I'm just tired of you ogling me all the time."

What the hell? "Jeez, woman, what got into you?" One minute she's humming, the next baring her teeth.

"You. That's what." She picked up the serving spoon and brandished it like a weapon. "All I am to you is a sexual fantasy."

Sky frowned. What she'd said wasn't true. Being around Pretty Windy was the worst kind of torture. Mostly because his feelings for her went beyond sexual. He cared about her. Cared? He was obsessed with her. She invaded every beat of his heart, every breath he took.

Sky raked his hands through his hair. What did all of that mean exactly? He'd never been obsessed with a woman before, never let one get under his skin. Had Cupid decided to play a trick on him and punish him for his sins? Had the mischievous matchmaker made the rotten cowboy fall for a woman he could never claim? A woman who would be repelled by his biggest sin?

Oh, hell, what did it matter? He'd never ask Windy to be a part of his life. He had nothing to offer a woman like her. He could dream about her until the moon turned blue, but it wouldn't change a thing.

"Aren't you going to answer me?" she snapped, jerking him from his disturbing thoughts.

"What am I supposed to say?"

"You could at least admit it's true." She waved the spoon again, sending spurts of liquid flying. "Do you think I like being told that all you think about is jumping my bones?"

How typically female, he thought. Now she was going to harp about something he'd said days ago. He considered accusing her of having PMS, but decided that would only tick her off even more. An apology, he supposed, was in order. He did follow her around the house like a rutting buck. "I'm sorry, okay? And you're not just a sexual fantasy to me." He forced out his next words, hating to admit them out loud. "I care about you."

Her eyes grew wide and kind of fluttery. "You do?"

Uh-oh. Time to change the subject. If she kept looking at him like that, he'd bare his Cupid-enhanced soul. He moved closer. "What's on the stove?"

She smiled. "Vegetable soup."

"It smells good."

"Do you want some?"

He rarely ate soup. Or vegetables. But after inadvertently provoking an argument, how could he refuse? "Yeah...sure."

Windy ladled the soup into a cup and handed it to him along with a spoon. He dipped into it and raised an odd-looking vegetable. The soup was filled with stuff he didn't recognize. He took a bite and swallowed quickly, not expecting to like it. Two spoonfuls later he decided it tasted as good as it smelled. "The big day's almost here, huh?"

She shrugged. "Just another birthday."

He'd been searching his rattled brain for the perfect gift, something personal, yet nonromantic. The last thing he wanted to do was allow her to guess how deep his feelings ran. He'd never given a woman a birthday gift before. He didn't do those kind of gestures well. But then, he'd never had to. Windy was the first woman who'd ever played havoc with his heart.

Sky finished the soup. "That was good. Don't recall if I've ever had homemade vegetable soup. Sure beats the canned stuff."

Windy smiled appreciatively. "Thanks." She took his empty cup and placed it in the sink. "Sky, I care about you, too."

"Yeah, I know." He glanced away then back again. "We're friends."

She twisted the ring on her finger, the one that had gotten tangled in his hair the day she'd nursed his bruises. The ruby was her birthstone, he surmised, wondering if it had been a gift from someone special.

"Sure, we're friends," she said, still turning the ring. "But I have to tell you the truth, Sky. I feel more for you than that."

Oh, no, he thought, fearful of what she might say. "Look, we've already established the fact that we've got this man-woman thing goin' on. There's no reason to beat it to death. We're attracted to each other, and sooner or later we'll get over it."

She exhaled a shaky-sounding breath. "I'm not sure I'll get over what I feel. Believe me, I've been trying to, but it's just not that easy."

Didn't he know it. Visions of her clouded his every thought. "Try a little harder, okay? Because I'm not up for this. And neither are you."

Tiny and determined in her summer cotton dress and messy ponytail, she stood her ground. The kitchen was her domain, he realized. Her sanctuary. If she needed to make a confession, it would be there, among the sparkling counters and red ging-ham.

"Sky," she said, meeting his wary gaze, "I know you're a loner and relationships have been difficult for you, but I think it's important for you to know that there are people who love—"

"Don't!" he shouted, then steadied his voice. "Please, Windy. Don't say it. Don't you dare tell me about all the people who love me." He raised his hand above his head. "I'm fed up to here with your psychology treatments. This orphan doesn't want to be loved."

Immediately her eyes glazed—a painful, teary glaze. He cursed his hurtful words but refused to take them back. If he explained why he didn't want her to love him, then he'd have to admit how he felt about her. And then the truth about his past would surface, and the terrible thing he had done to a child who needed him. He wasn't ready for Windy to hate him yet. Maybe he'd never be ready. Maybe he'd rather leave knowing someone did love him—someone decent and kind and pure.

"I gotta get out of here." He strode from the kitchen to the front door without looking back. He needed to be alone in his

misery. Solitude he could handle. He'd been alone all of his
life.

At 3:00 a.m. Windy paced the length of the kitchen, a cord-
less phone cradled against her ear. "I'm so worried." How
many times had she said that to Edith tonight? And how many
hours had they been on the phone? "The bars closed at two.
Where could he be?"

Edith's tone was quiet, patient. "Skyler's a grown man,
dear. He can take care of himself."

"But you didn't see his face when I tried to tell him how
I feel about him." He'd looked almost afraid, she thought.
Afraid and angry. "He said he was tired of my psychology
treatments, but I wasn't—"

"I know. You fell in love with him, and it's your nature to
help people. You didn't do or say anything wrong."

Windy blinked back the tears threatening her eyes. "What
if he doesn't come home?" Maybe he'd just drift out of her
life. Disappear for good. He didn't want her to love him. He'd
said so.

"He'll be back," the other woman assured. "He had promised to stay with you until September, and he will."

Windy sat at the table and stared at the herb tea she'd
brewed but hadn't been able to drink. Sky might walk out on
her, but he wouldn't leave Tequila. That snake had been a part
of his life for too many years for him to abandon it. She knew
how difficult it had been for him to put a lock on Tequila's
cage. Edith was right. He'd be back. He would never leave
Tequila with her; she was still afraid of the enormous reptile.

"This waiting is driving me crazy," she said. "Dang it,
where could he be?"

"Alone somewhere, I would imagine," Edith responded
with a sigh. "I doubt Sky has ever been involved in an emotional relationship before. You're going to have to give him
some time to adjust."

"I know." Windy hadn't planned on telling Sky how she
felt. It just happened. And it hadn't even been an outright

admission. She had only implied that she loved him, yet he'd become enraged, anyway. "I'm new at this too, Edith. He's the first man I've ever been in love with."

"Being in love is wonderful, dear. But it can be overwhelming, too. I enjoyed being married, but my husband, God rest his soul, was a difficult man at times. I suppose it had something to do with the difference between men and women. We never seemed to understand each other." Edith clucked her tongue.

"Oh, God…I hear someone outside. I think he might be home." Windy rushed into the living room and stared at the front door. The jangle of keys jolted her frantic heart. When the doorknob turned, she caught her breath. "It's him."

"Okay." Relief sounded in Edith's voice. "Remember, give him some time. And if either of you need me, I'll be home tomorrow."

"Thanks. Bye." She pushed the power button on the phone and stared at the man standing at the front door.

"Hi." She placed the phone on the coffee table. "Are you all right?"

He took a step forward then proceeded to the couch, where he glanced down at the coffee table. "Who were you talking to?"

"Edith."

He dropped his head back as though extremely tired. Or intoxicated. "You shouldn't have brought her into this."

"I needed someone to talk to. Are you drunk?"

He lifted his head. "No."

"I thought maybe you'd been to a bar. It's so late, and I kept wondering where you'd gone."

He pulled his hand through his hair. He looked unkempt, wind tousled and wrinkled. His shirt was untucked, and the bottom of his jeans cuffed with dirt. "Is that your way of asking me where I've been?"

It was, she supposed, but she hated to admit it. "You were upset when you left. Once it got so late, I was worried you might have gone to a bar and gotten into a fight."

"I went for a long drive. Ended up at the beach."

That explained the dirt on his jeans—moist sand. "So you stood near the water and watched the tide come in?"

"Yeah. It was a quiet place to think."

She remained in the center of her own living room, feeling uncomfortable. Sky seemed like such a stranger now, someone she couldn't communicate with. If she asked him what he'd been thinking about, he'd probably accuse her of trying to conduct a therapy session. It hurt that he kept throwing her psychology training back in her face. It made her feel as if he was trying to discredit her. "Edith said she'd be home tomorrow if you need anything."

He removed his boots and placed them under the coffee table. "I couldn't talk to her about this."

Windy took a tentative step closer. "Can you talk to me?"

"I suppose I'll have to since it concerns you."

That flapjack sensation started flipping her stomach again. She didn't want to push him, yet she needed to repair the emotional devastation between them. She couldn't apologize for her admission, though. She wasn't sorry she'd fallen in love with him.

Windy moved toward the couch then sat beside him, gauging Sky's response. She prayed his posture wouldn't stiffen, or his eyes wouldn't turn hard. The rejection would kill her. He'd already broken a piece of her heart today. She couldn't take much more.

He looked her way. His eyes weren't hard, but they were cautious, she noticed. A wary shade of blue. "I still don't like L.A.," he said.

She swallowed. "Does that mean you're moving sooner than you'd anticipated?"

"No. It means just because I spent some quality time at the beach, my opinion of the city hasn't changed." He heaved a masculine sigh. "I figured out why I've been so sexual with you, and it's not the celibacy."

She would have preferred hearing about love rather than sex, but she sat patiently, waiting for him to continue.

"I've never been attracted to a woman who's so moral. Who's actually saving herself for the right guy." He looked up at the ceiling then at the coffee table, as though momentarily avoiding her gaze. "It's making me a little crazy."

Windy didn't understand. "You're going to have to explain that one."

"Yeah, I suppose I am." This time he looked directly at her. "I think I'm jealous of the guy who will eventually get you." The corners of his mouth formed a sad smile. "My imagination goes nuts, envisioning you with someone else, knowing he's going to do the things to you that I want to do."

She didn't dare ask about those things, although she wanted to know. Her imagination had been going crazy with fantasies of him. "There's more to a relationship than the physical side."

"I know. And that's where the rest of my explanation comes in." He exhaled one long, heavy breath. "There's a part of me that wonders what it would be like to be the guy you've been saving yourself for—to be that special to you. I know you claim to have feelings for me, but we both know there's no future for us. It's foolish for either of us to dream about what's never going to be."

Windy's heart all but melted. He does want to be loved, she thought, and he wants to love back. He just doesn't know how. She studied his eyes, the longing and the need. Sky was fighting his emotions. Windy realized she meant more to him than a wistful sexual partner. Sky had begun to fall in love with her, and the unfamiliar feeling frightened him.

"We've only known each other for a little over a month," she said, taking care with her words. She would give him time, just as Edith had suggested. "It's too soon to talk about a future."

"I'm leaving in September, Windy."

"I know, but we can keep in touch," she said, although that wasn't the sentiment in her heart. She wanted him to live with her forever.

"Where do you plan on going?" she asked.

He shrugged. ''I don't usually make plans. And it depends on how much of my memory returns, or if it ever does.''

''You'd like to search for your roots.''

''Yeah, something like that.'' He stood and rolled his shoulders, appearing even more exhausted. ''I'm gonna get some sleep.'' He leaned forward and touched one of her renegade curls. ''I'm sorry I made you worry, Pretty Windy. And I'm sorry if I hurt you. I didn't mean to, it's just…well, you know.''

Yes, she knew. She sent him a gentle smile and watched him head down the hall. He loved her. In his own tortured way—Sky loved her.

Windy placed her hand against her heart, felt the beats intensify. She would not let Skyler go, not now that she knew he was falling in love with her. Somehow, some way, she would keep him, convince him to stay.

Windy headed to her own room, her steps light. Tonight she would dream of happily ever after. And before September she would make that dream come true.

Eleven

Another year older, Windy thought as she gazed at her reflection. She stood in her bedroom, dressed in a cream-colored silk blouse and pleated pants—her going-out-with-a-girlfriend look. Comfortable yet stylish.

A knock sounded and she smiled. It had to be Sky. She opened the door.

"Hi." He stood there grinning boyishly, a small box in his hand. "Happy birthday."

"Thank you." She glanced down at the wrapped package. "Is that for me?"

"Uh-huh." He handed her the gift and walked into her room.

Windy held the brightly wrapped package. "You already baked me a cake. You didn't have to get me something, too." Edith had arrived earlier that day with a delicious chocolate cake in tow, claiming Sky had helped bake it.

Both of his dimples surfaced. "Edith did most of the work. Pretty much all I did was lick the spoon."

She laughed, adoring his smile and the dimples that endeared it. "Well, it's the thought that counts."

"You look nice," he said, examining her appearance. "I like your top. It suits you."

"Thanks." The silk blouse boasted a simple adornment: tiny gold buttons. "It's one of my favorites, too." She touched the glossy red bow on the gift he'd given her. Her heart lunged. "Can I open this now?"

"Sure. It's your present."

Windy sat on the edge of her bed and removed the bow from atop the box. "I recycle bows and ribbons," she said. "It's such a waste to throw them away when it's so easy to use them again."

He arched one black eyebrow. "You don't save the paper, too, do you?"

"No." She grinned and tore off the wrapping, then opened the jewelry-style box. Her heart skipped an excited beat. A flash of gold sparkled: a delicate ID bracelet. She lifted the bracelet off the cotton pad, jangled the chain, then brought the smooth plate forward to read the inscription: *"Hērus Hotv ́letv."*

Windy looked up at Sky.

"It means Pretty Windy in the Muskokee language," he explained.

She traced the words with her finger and gazed at him through blurred vision. Tears had already begun to collect in her eyes. She wanted to throw her arms around him and kiss him breathless, taste his tongue, run her hands through his midnight hair. "Thank you. This is beautiful. You are such a special man."

Although he shrugged, he smiled, clearly pleased with her emotional response. "There's an inscription on the back, too."

Turning the bracelet over she discovered a smaller script that read: "Happy birthday, Love, Sútv."

"So this is your name in Muskokee?"

He nodded. "It's pronounced Sootuh."

She secured the bracelet around her wrist and studied the

front inscription again: *"Hếrus Hotv'letv."* "How do you say Pretty Windy?"

"Heroos Hotuh-letuh," he said, making her Muskokee name sound guttural and sexy. "In Windy, the *V* translates like a short English *U,* as in *but.*"

And the *O* was long, she noticed, and the *E* short. "Do you remember this from your childhood?"

"No. I bought a Muskokee dictionary to see if any of the words were familiar. The only one that struck a chord was *Sútv*—Sky. Maybe my parents used to call me by my Creek name once in a while."

Windy smiled. It was an exotic, beautiful name, she thought, just like the man. "Where are the Creeks from?"

"They started off in Georgia and Alabama, but were moved to Indian Territory in Oklahoma in the winter of 1836 and '37."

"So you might be from Oklahoma?"

"Seems likely, but not all the Creek population still lives there. And until I remember what my real last name is, there's no point in trying to second-guess where I came from."

Windy stood and moved closer to him. "Thank you again for the bracelet. I'll never take it off."

"Good." He skimmed a calloused finger across her cheek. "Then I'll know that you'll never forget about me."

And that was the idea, she realized. He'd given her a gift to remember him by, and the Creek names engraved upon it made it especially personal. Forget about him? That wasn't possible. She'd love him until her dying day. And she wanted him. Now. On her birthday. In her bed.

The jungle-printed allure of her room cried out for him. He belonged amid the other wild creatures—the paintings of panthers and lions, the faux leopard quilt and zebra pillows. A tingle shivered her spine. All she had to do was step closer and kiss him. Unbutton his denim shirt, caress that bronze chest, press her hips against the front of those faded jeans.

Seduce him, a voice in her head whispered.

Windy smiled. Yes, she would seduce him. Late tonight, in

her room with moonlight dancing across the bed. She wanted to be Skyler's lover, helpmate and lifelong partner.

"Enjoy your birthday celebration," he said.

"What?"

"With your teacher friend."

"Oh, I will," she answered, certain this would be the most incredible night of her life.

When Windy arrived home late that evening, she soaked in a tub filled with vanilla-scented bath oil, covered a new baby-doll nightie with a matching silk robe and headed straight for Tequila's cage before she lost her nerve. She intended to seduce Sky without him knowing it was intentional. After all, they had shared a bed the last time the snake was loose. So why not tonight?

"All right." She breathed heavily and peered into the snake's domain. "Here goes."

With a catch in her throat, she removed the metal bolt, placed her hands on the screened top of the terrarium and lifted it as quickly as possible. The curious gray reptile raised itself to inspect the open space. Windy cringed and jumped back.

Poised at the rim of the container, Tequila flicked her tongue steadily as she lifted her striped head. *Oh, no.* Windy wrung her hands together as the snake slid from the cage and moved in a slow but determined manner toward her.

Remaining perfectly still, she watched five feet of dark gray muscle-mass coil around her bare feet. Quiet, she told herself. Stay calm. Stay quiet. The plans she had for this evening did not include screaming like a banshee.

"Go away," she whispered in a stiff voice, remembering Sky had said this friendly reptile understood English. Or was it Spanish?

Since English was the only language Windy knew, and this enormous beast looked much too content at her feet, she pleaded with it. "Please, Tequila, go away. Go hide."

Instead of departing, the friendly snake raised itself to test the hem of Windy's flowing robe with the top of its head. If she climbs up my leg, I'll die. Faint dead away. When Windy heard Sky's husky but groggy voice, she knew this brilliant plan was sinking fast.

He stumbled into the living room wearing a pair of button fly jeans, not quite buttoned. "What's going on out here?"

She feigned innocence. "Tequila got loose."

Sky looked down at her feet, and Windy knew he struggled not to laugh. How very like him, she thought. Here she stood a failed seductress, and he had the audacity to be amused.

He moved closer. "Hmm. I wonder how Tequila managed to knock that bolt out of place. I'm sure it was secure."

Oh, good grief. "I don't know, but do you think you could get her away from me?" Windy asked in a voice wavering on hysteria. By now Tequila had decided to share a warm spot inside her robe.

With a slight grin, Sky plopped himself down on the floor next to the snake.

"Nice robe." He reached underneath, removed the snake's curious head and brushed a calloused hand against Windy's leg.

Tequila went slithering back to her cage, but Sky didn't move. He remained on his knees, at Windy's feet. The belt dangling from her robe caught his attention. With a mischievous grin, he pulled it. The peach garment fluttered before it opened.

Windy shuddered as Sky's hands traveled up her bare legs, caressing their way to her thighs. "Tell me why you opened Tequila's cage," he said, toying with the lace hem on her nightie.

"You know why." Surely he must have figured it out. He must have seen her lift the top on the cage.

"Say it. I need to hear you say it."

"Oh...I..." She looked down to see him looking up. An enigmatic smile and two dangerous blue eyes seemed to be awaiting their feminine feast. A current of electricity ripped through her. "I was hoping you'd sleep in my room."

"Why?" The smile widened, baring white teeth that seemed eager to nip.

"Because I want you to make love to me." Her breathy response brought Sky to his feet.

"Pretty, Pretty Windy," he whispered, as he lifted the hem of her skimpy nightgown, and rubbed the hard ridge in his jeans back and forth over her panties.

He tilted his head and captured her lips, seeking the kiss they both ached for. Instinctively Windy rose on her toes and reached up to touch him. Moving closer, she traced the arch of his brow, the hollow of his cheek, the hard angle of his jaw, wanting—no, *needing*—to explore every nuance of him. Their tongues mated frantically. For too long they had denied their passion, and now all at once they tried to sate a hunger that burned madly out of control. The kiss was hot and searing, the rhythm of his hips making it even more so.

"Windy." Sky pulled away with a slight groan. "If we do this— I can't make a commitment. Nothing's changed…I can't promise any kind of future."

"I understand." What he said hardly mattered because she knew he loved her. Deep in the recess of his mind, he loved her. And she loved him. "I want you to be my first."

He touched her cheek, then pulled back a little. "I wasn't expecting this to happen between us. I don't keep any protection around. It's just been so long since I've been with anyone. And I won't…we can't without—" He sounded as if he were apologizing for not being prepared for her seduction. "I don't suppose you—"

She placed her palms flat against his naked chest, and he sucked in a barely controlled breath. "I bought some tonight, Sky. And I want to be your lover, more than I've ever wanted anything."

He leaned in and covered her mouth with his, acknowledging her admission with a scorching kiss. Then he raised his fingers to her nightgown, sending butterfly touches across her breasts, circling the hardened nipples, rubbing the fabric against her aching flesh.

When the kiss ended, he dropped his chin and slid his tongue down the valley between her breasts and pushed the robe off her shoulders. It fell to the floor in a rippling pool of peach silk. The baby doll nightie came next, adding lace and ribbon to the silk pond. He began bathing her, teasing the rosy crest of one nipple with his tongue. And then he was tugging and suckling so fiercely she cried out in a frenzied moan.

She dizzied from the feel of him, the warmth of his breath, tease of his tongue, ripple of muscle cording his back. When he lifted his head, Windy reached into his hair, seized his scalp, and pulled him toward her other breast. The quiet laugh from his throat sounded low and sinfully wicked as he lowered his mouth to give her the pleasure she craved.

Windy wasn't sure how or when it happened, but she found herself straddling him, her legs locked around his hips as he whisked her down the hall.

He dived, and they landed on her bed together, arms and legs flying, yellow and black hair tangling as they kissed.

"Handsome *Sútv*." Windy wanted to tell him how much she loved him. Instead, she opened the top drawer of her dresser, removed the condom box and told him how much she needed him.

"Show *Sútv* how much you need him," he teased, rolling her over until she sat across his hips.

Windy reached into the waistband of her panties, and removed the last of her wispy clothing. Feeling shy or awkward had no place in her mind. Tonight there was only the feel of the man she loved—the emotion of wanting to experience him. Studying the rise in his partially unbuttoned jeans, she rocked her hips. "Your turn to show me how much you need me."

In one quick roll she was beneath him. "It's my turn to kiss you," he said, pushing his tongue into her mouth and covering her naked body with his hands. Windy felt him everywhere. Touching, caressing, exploring. A contradiction of sensation engulfed her. Her limbs seemed molten, yet her heart pulsed with life, strong and steady, pumping heat through her veins.

When he slipped a finger into her moist center, she arched against his hand. "Pretty, wild Windy." His voice seduced as his finger delved deeper. "I want to make you scream."

She watched, anticipating as his lips blazed a trail down her body. He nuzzled the fullness of her breasts, slid his mouth down her rib cage, kissed the hard points of her hip bones. And then he paused at her thighs to look up at her.

His gaze was too vibrant, too arresting. A cobalt fire ignited within her. She closed her eyes. A soft moan escaped her lips as he parted her thighs. She tensed, caught her breath and a choked cry with it. The tip of his tongue was taking, giving, dipping sensuously into the essence of her femininity.

With slow, mounting strokes, he tasted, then savored, each deliberate laving spreading through her like a searing flame. Grasping her hips, he found her core and pulled her closer.

She shuddered.

He suckled.

She screamed.

As she shook through a series of cataclysmic convulsions, he made her cry his name out loud, over and over, until those three simple letters branded her heart.

"Oh, Sky." Windy kissed his smiling lips and melted against him, the power of his body absorbing the last ripple of her orgasm.

His smile increased. "I love touching you…watching you." He wrapped her in his arms. "And I love hearing you say my name." He took her hand and moved it up and down, over the bulge stretching his jeans. "Say my name."

She reached into the denim fly and worked free the last three buttons. "Sky." The first one popped. "Sky." The second one. After the third, she skimmed the sensitive tip of his erection.

Together, they pushed his jeans down. Shoving them away, he invited her to embrace him. "Please, Windy, touch me. Put your hands…"

Answering his carnal plea, she encircled him, and he surged, hot and greedy into her palm. With each insistent stroke, she pushed her fingers upward, urging him to move within her grasp. As he did, he mumbled her name in his native tongue. The low guttural sound filled the room—a sound that made her want him even more.

As he braced himself above her, his hair fell forward. "Are you ready?" he asked, as though desperate to be a part of her.

She reached up to touch his face, his hair, the muscles in his neck. She wanted to know all of him, every feature, every pore, the knife-blade ridge of his cheekbones, the moist feel of his lips, the cut of his jaw. "Yes," she whispered. "I'm ready."

He opened one of the foil packets, then took her hand and encouraged her to touch him again, to stroke him before protecting them both.

He nuzzled her hair and, within seconds, they feasted on each other's mouths, hungry and anxious. She placed her lips against his throat while he entered her, feeling his erratic pulse. She clawed his back as the first thrust of pain burst through her body, then lifted her hips when it turned to a needy ache.

He drove her slowly at first, rocking her, introducing her to his dance, to the silky rhythm of lovemaking. The mosquito netting draped above her bed provided a hazy film, a curtain of exotic ambience. It didn't matter that Sky wasn't her husband, or this wasn't her honeymoon. The wedding night of her dreams couldn't compare to the beauty of Sky's body filling hers. He had a warrior's body, tall and powerful. And his eyes, a blazing shade of blue, stared into hers. He was, without a doubt, the man she loved.

Sky pushed his hands through her hair, spilling curls over her shoulders and across the pillow. "You're perfect, Pretty Windy." He buried himself deeper and groaned. "So perfect."

She gasped, certain she would crave him every night. Every hour. Every minute. She would never get enough of his hard, virile body or long, tapered fingers. Or that mouth suckling her nipple—that moist, luscious mouth. Every movement, every hurried, eager touch brought a fresh thrill. A raw, wicked thrill.

She dragged his lips to hers, and they coupled passionately. She raised her hips as his lowered, meeting his powerful thrusts with the same vigorous rhythm. The flesh that ignited was bronzed and fair, rough and smooth, swollen and moist. The nails that clawed were hers, the teeth that nipped, his. When the climax came, it was shared through a violent storm of lust and need—a combination so strong and new, when it ended, tears sprang from her eyes.

As Windy clutched his head to her breast, Sky basked in her warmth. Such a special lady, he thought. So pure and delicate. Never had he imagined being offered the gift of a woman's virginity.

He peered up at her, ready to ask if the experience made her feel changed in any way, but when he saw her fragile expression, a jolt of fear ripped through him. Fresh tears spiked her lashes.

Had he been too rough, or did she suddenly regret the choice she'd made? Were those tears of sorrow? Remorse?

Sky positioned himself above her. She looked soft and angelic, her golden hair fanned around her like a halo. "Did I hurt you?"

She ran her fingertips along his jaw. "There was a little pain at first, but not later."

He swallowed. "Then why are you crying?"

"Oh." She rubbed her cheeks with the back of her hand. "I didn't mean to." She blinked, fluttering her glistening lashes. "Sometimes I cry when I'm happy."

Sky's heart leaped into his throat. "Then you don't regret what we did?"

"No." Her eyes grew wide and fearful. "Do you?"

Relieved, he kissed the tip of her nose. Sweet Windy. His virgin angel. His summer love. "No." He should, he supposed, but their joining had felt too perfect for regrets. Sky made a silent promise to treat her honorably. And he would start right now. "Close your eyes, Windy. I'll be right back."

He padded to the bathroom and returned with a basin of warm water and a soft cloth. He placed the water on the nightstand and sat beside her. He intended to care for her, bathe her the way a warrior should.

Apparently aware of his purpose, she reached for the cloth. "I can…"

"Let me." He cradled her in his arms and cleansed her gently, wiping the maiden's blood from her thighs. "This is ceremonial in my culture," he told her, hoping to ease her shyness. She hadn't been shy during their loving, but this, he knew, was even more intimate.

"Okay." She buried her head against his shoulder. "I'm so glad it was you, Sky."

"Me, too." He wondered if it would sound strange to thank her. Somehow those words didn't seem strong enough to express what he felt. She had thought enough of him to give herself freely, to let him share her body for the first time. How could he thank her for that? A woman he would walk away from?

Sky finished bathing her, allowing her a quiet moment to relax. Even if he wanted to stay, he couldn't. Their union was meant to be just what it was—a warm, sexy, summer breeze. She would find someone else someday, and he would search for his past—a past that shamed him.

He glanced at the clock. They had made love on her birthday, and she was in his arms, naked, except for the gold bracelet he had given her. No, he realized, reaching for her hand, that wasn't true. She wore the ruby ring as well.

"It was a gift from my mother," she said.

"I wasn't going to ask."

"But I could tell you wondered."

He held her hand, rubbed his fingers over the half-moons on her nails. Someday a man would give her a ring, he thought. A wedding band. Damn it. Sky inhaled a heavy breath. He missed her already and they were still together. He'd find out, of course, when she married. Once he was gone, he'd ask Edith about her.

She nuzzled closer. "It's been such a wonderful day."

He smiled. "Birthdays are supposed to be happy."

"You know what I was thinking?" she asked.

He stroked her hair. "What?"

"That I've never seen you perform." She skimmed her fingers along his jaw. "I want to visit Rodeo Knights, see the beautiful Skyler in action."

Beautiful? He couldn't resist a chuckle. Flashy was more like it. He wore an array of Western garb during his solo that could blind a seeing-eye dog. Of course, he'd gotten used to the rhinestone-cowboy act, at least in the arena. He wouldn't be caught dead in satin and fringe otherwise. Simple ranch wear was more his style, but he was good at what he did. Trick riding came natural. Someday, though, he'd be ready to give it up and buy himself some acreage, breed and train horses.

Yeah, right. Sky brought Windy closer. Did he honestly think he would be able to settle down? Quit running from his past? Finding his son might be next to impossible, and even if he did locate the boy, the kid might hate him.

Don't think about that now, he told himself. Tonight he needed to focus on the woman in his arms. They had less than eight weeks to be together. "I'd love for you to come to one of the shows," he said. "And afterward you can hang out in my dressing room."

"My, my," she teased. "The man has his own dressing room."

"Don't get too impressed. It's dinky. Not much bigger than a walk-in closet. And the only reason I was offered a little privacy is because I know the boss so well."

Windy drew the sheet up, covering them both. "Since I'll be visiting you at work, maybe you could visit me one day, too."

Sky tried not to wince. "You mean at the preschool?" Little children with big, hopeful eyes made him feel like a monster inside. He still had nightmares about abandoning his son. God, how could he have left an innocent child? "I don't know,

Windy. I mean, what would I do at a preschool all day? I'd be in the way.''

She gazed up at him. "You could visit during Career Week. The kids would be thrilled to meet a professional cowboy. Heck, half the boys want to be cowboys, anyway.''

Preschool children, tiny trusting souls. Lord help him. "Aren't they a mite young to be thinking about a career?''

"Three- and four-year-olds love to playact and imagine themselves as adults. Besides, this helps them understand what kind of work their parents do and how important everyone's job is.'' She cuddled closer. Clearly a feminine ploy to lure him into her trap. "So far we have a nurse, a grocery checker and a fireman who have agreed to visit. A real-live cowboy would sure be nice.''

He frowned. "Can I think about it?''

"No problem.'' She kissed his scowl, slowly coaxing a smile. "Career Week isn't until next month.''

He slid his hands up her spine, felt her nipples harden against his chest. Damn she was gorgeous. A tumbling blonde with a sweet vanilla scent and an adoring expression.

Windy licked his bottom lip, then closed her hand over his erection. Sky kept his eyes on hers while she experimented, innocently seducing the hell out of him. Go ahead, he thought. Wrap me in your tender web. Make me forget about how undeserving I am.

Although the lamp beside the bed burned low, moonlight filtered through the windows, illuminating the animal prints with a misty glow. Time stood still as their mouths came together, and all at once the taste of her spilled into his soul.

Yes, he thought again, as his heart rammed against hers. Devour me. Love me madly. At least until September.

Twelve

What a glorious morning, Windy thought. She placed the breakfast tray on the nightstand and opened the curtains. Sunlight danced upon Sky's hair, turning the black locks a midnight shade of blue. His eyelids fluttered against his cheeks while he slept, his breaths even and low. The top sheet was tangled around his waist, the quilt pushed to the end of the bed.

They had made love last night. Twice. And then they had cuddled spoon-style, her back to his front, the way first-time lovers should. She couldn't have dreamed up a more romantic evening, or a more giving partner.

She touched Sky's cheek, gliding her fingers over the rasp of beard stubble. "Hey, sleepyhead."

He roused with a groan, opened each eye slowly, squinted, peered at her, then quirked a lazy smile. "Hey, yourself, pretty lady."

Windy's heart skipped a satisfied beat. A naked male stirring in her bed—lean muscles, blue eyes and flickering dimples. What more could a woman want?

Forever, her mind answered. A lifetime with him. "I made breakfast."

He sniffed the air, turned toward the aroma. "Cinnamon rolls. What did I do to rate fresh-baked pastries at—" pausing, he spied the clock "—eleven?" He sat up, rolled his shoulders. "Damn, I slept in."

"There's coffee, too," she said, handing him a cup. "And what you did was give me the best night of my life."

He grinned, then sipped the hot drink. "An A-plus performance, huh, teach? Will I get a report card? Maybe a gold star?"

She smiled back, realizing her compliment had embarrassed him a little. His grin had a shyness attached. "How about a kiss instead?"

They exchanged a gentle kiss over the rim of his steaming coffee—a comfortable, familiar kiss, a greeting of contented lovers. Windy melted during every minute of it, the tenderness, the warmth, the taste of caffeine and man.

He sat back and sipped his coffee again.

"Is there enough sugar?" she asked.

"Yeah, it's sweet, just like the lady who brewed it." Reaching across the nightstand, he snagged a cinnamon roll. "I've gotta have one of these." He took one generous bite, moaning approval as he ate. "Did the phone ring earlier? Or was I dreaming? Could of sworn I heard bells."

Out of habit, she handed him a napkin. "That was a few hours ago, but it was an important call—"

"Was it Lucy?" Sky asked. "Is she leaving Hank?"

"It wasn't her." Windy knew he still worried about the frail young woman, hoped, as she did, that Lucy would seek the help they'd offered. "It was Officer Mallory. They arrested the boys who vandalized this place. Seems they hit another house last night and got caught." Mere children, she thought. Troubled teens. "They admitted they were the ones who had vandalized the other homes in the area."

Sky placed his coffee on the nightstand. "God, that was an important call. So how many boys were involved?"

"Two. And they're only fourteen. Just babies. I can't imagine what provoked them to do something like that. Officer Mallory said they come from wealthy families. Spoiled rich kids out for kicks, but I think there's probably more to it."

Sky shook his head. "Don't you dare feel sorry for those brats, Windy. What kind of kids would deliberately terrorize single young women? What they did scared the hell out of you."

"I know. And I don't feel sorry for them, but I can't help but worry." Someone, she thought, had to make sure the youth of today got help. "Their families offered to pay for all the damages, but I suppose that would have come up in the hearing, anyway." She lifted her tea. "I wonder if they did it to get their parents' attention, or if it's something else they're acting out."

"I don't know, but you're not going to find out. Promise me you won't get involved in this one, Windy. Let the law handle it." He reached for her hand. "They don't deserve a sweet girl like you worrying about them."

Although Officer Mallory had assured her the boys would be punished by the juvenile court system, he also set her fears to rest that they'd be evaluated by a court-appointed psychologist. And as one of their victims, if she had anything to say about it, she'd insist on counseling.

She squeezed Sky's hand. "I won't involve myself as anything more than a victim invoking her rights, okay?"

"Okay." He breathed a relieved sigh. "Boy, I'm so glad the police caught them. I couldn't have left here knowing those vandals were still out there."

Immediately pain and fear flooded her heart. She had less than two months to convince Sky to stay, convince him what domestic bliss could be like. Baking pastries was a start, a small one, but a start just the same. Visiting Rodeo Knights would be another. If they were going to continue being lovers, then they should know everything about each other, including their jobs. She wanted him to visit her at the preschool, too. She knew her kids would adore him, and Sky needed that kind of social acceptance. He seemed to think small children would fear him. Windy intended to prove that ludicrous theory wrong.

She picked up her coffee. Could she really convince him to stay? He hated California. She sipped the warm brew, her mind working into overdrive. Maybe he only hated California because it reminded him of the accident, of the day he'd lost his memory. What he needed were new memories—lazy, happy days in California with the woman he loved. Strolls along the beach, home-cooked meals, afternoons on horseback, warm summer nights making slow, torturous love.

It was worth a try, she thought. She wanted Sky more than she had ever wanted anything in her life. And he loved her— not just with his body, but with his heart. Maybe he didn't quite know it yet, but he would. The more time they spent together, he would figure it out. And then he'd accept her loving him. She hoped.

Windy chewed her bottom lip. What else was missing? What detail had she forgotten?

Oh, goodness. As last night's seduction filled her mind, the answer came plain as day.

Tequila. The snake.

If she was going to win Sky's trust, then she'd have to tolerate that beast. Tequila was, after all, his spirit animal— an important aspect of his life.

Windy glanced over at Sky. Could she do it? Be comfortable around a snake? A huge, slimy creature with beady eyes and fangs?

Yes, she told herself nervously. She could. Especially if it meant making herself invaluable to the man she loved.

Windy drew a deep breath, then forced out her next words. "Sky, I think you should leave Tequila's cage unlocked from now on."

His jaw nearly dropped. "You do? I thought you were scared of her."

False bravado kept her voice steady. "Not really. Not any-more. I mean, I think I could get used to her." *As long as she leaves me alone.*

He chuckled. "You looked pretty scared of her last night."

"It wasn't fear exactly," she lied. "It was more like…well, embarrassment, I suppose. She was ruining my seduction."

He moved closer, reached for her robe. "How about we try that scenario again? Only this time you get to seduce me in the shower."

Yum, she thought. Soapy hands, pelting water and warm, aroused bodies. "Maybe."

"Maybe?" he parroted, stroking her nipple through the satin robe. "What's that supposed to mean?"

She struggled to keep herself afloat, to stay focused on her sudden idea. His fingers on her sensitive nipple had her head reeling. "It means," she said, gently removing his hand, "that if you agree to participate in Career Week at the preschool, I'll seduce you wherever and whenever you want."

His eyebrows shot up. "I thought I had time to think about it."

Reveling in her newfound power, Windy scraped her nails down his chest. "You do. Only, I thought if you wanted to strike a bargain," she said, lowering her lashes in feigned innocence, "we could take a shower together every morning."

He swallowed. "This is blackmail."

"Is it?" she asked. "Why, it's just a shower, Sky. A little soap and water." She smiled at his tortured expression. "I don't see the big deal."

"Really?" He brought his face next to hers, tangled his hands in her sleep-tossed hair. "Ever since that day you made me stand guard in the bathroom, I've had this fantasy about us…in the shower—" he nibbled her ear "—naked, our mouths…our tongues…"

Oh, my. "Career Week," she whispered back, on the verge of jumping into his lap and straddling him with one greedy thrust. Struggling for control, she ran her lips across his, tasting his fever. His need. His resolve.

He plunged his tongue into her mouth and lifted her off the bed.

"You win," he growled, carrying her to the shower. "Damn it, you win."

They kissed and groped beneath the spray of water, looked into each other's eyes and made love in a fury of passion, a maelstrom of need. And when they slid to the porcelain, sated yet spent, Sky cursed. Neither, it seemed, had remembered the protection.

Two days later Windy flung the front door open. "Oh, thank goodness, you're here!" she exclaimed with nervous relief when she saw Melissa. "Tequila has been following me around all evening. I've been so scared. I didn't know who else to call."

Calling Sky was out of the question. He didn't have the kind of job where he could drop everything and come home. Besides, he would only remind her that leaving Tequila's cage unlocked had been her idea. Windy glanced down at the snake. What in the world had possessed her to think she could tolerate a five-foot reptile? Or that it would make a difference in her relationship with Sky? All she wanted to do was get the enormous beast back into its cage.

Melissa wore an expression of genuine sympathy. "My mom didn't mind dropping me off. And she would have come in to help, but she doesn't like snakes."

Smart woman, Windy thought. "Melissa, do you think you're strong enough to get Tequila away from me?"

"Sure." The young girl bent down to pick up the snake, but when she tried to lift the huge beast, Tequila tightened her grip around Windy's ankles.

"Oh, my God." Windy moaned. "Now what?"

"Just stay calm," Melissa cautioned. "She won't hurt you. I think she's trying to be your friend."

Windy looked down at the gray reptile. "Well, some fine way to be someone's friend. She hasn't left me alone since I came home from work. She wouldn't even let me go to the bathroom by myself. Can you believe she followed me in there?'' It amazed Windy how swiftly the snake could move when it chose to. "I mean, okay, I thought I could get used to having her around. But not like this.''

The twelve-year-old cracked a girlish giggle. Apparently the bathroom scenario was too much.

Windy shook her head and smiled, embarrassed by her own admission. "It wasn't funny at the time, but I suppose it is now.''

"Maybe you better try to make friends with her. I don't think she's going to leave you alone until you do.'' Melissa spoke like the true mediator she was. Windy knew the young girl had a knack for bringing people together. Of course, this was probably the first time she ever had to mediate for a snake.

"What should I do?'' Windy wiggled her leg, noticing Tequila had loosened her grip.

"Can you walk to the couch?'' the girl asked, holding out a hand to help. "You look sort of pale.''

With Melissa's aid, Windy made her way to the couch, carefully stepping around Tequila's coiled form. She feared one false move would prompt the boa to strike.

The moment Windy eased herself onto the couch, Tequila climbed onto her lap.

"Now, just stay calm,'' Melissa cautioned once again. "Remember, she just wants to be friends.''

"Are you sure?'' Windy asked stiffly. The snake looked vicious up close. Sneaky and dangerous.

"You should pet her.'' Melissa moved closer for support, then reached out to stroke the snake. "See, she likes it.''

Windy's arm bristled with goose bumps. Could she actually touch that slimy thing? "I don't know.''

"We'll pet her together,'' the girl offered.

All right, Windy told herself. Just do it. Get it over with. Be brave. She may as well get to know the annoying boa. After all, the snake and Sky were a package deal.

She raised her hand cautiously, looking for the end without teeth. At the moment Tequila's head was tucked into a fold of her oversize T-shirt, making the reptile look like one continuous, winding gray mass.

Melissa kept her promise and reached out, coaxing Windy to do the same.

"Wow." Windy was awestruck. She had expected its skin to feel wet and slimy or rough and scaly. But Tequila was as smooth as silk. Instinctively, she traced the length of the reptile, marveling at its beauty. An overwhelming feeling of pride came over her, realizing the unrelenting effort it took on Tequila's part to capture her attention.

This was a good sign, she thought. Tequila had accepted her as Sky's mate. And since the snake had supposedly sent Windy that spiritual dream, maybe Sky would realize that he and Windy were meant to be together from the beginning, that Tequila had been right all along.

Melissa smiled. "I told you she just wanted to be friends."

"And you were right," Windy responded as her stomach growled. She grinned at Melissa. "Sorry, I haven't eaten since lunch. I'm starving."

"Me, too." Melissa hopped off the couch. "Let's go fix a snack."

"Okay." Oh, goodness, now she felt guilty about disturbing Tequila. The friendly snake looked so content on her lap. "Tequila." She poked the still gray form. "I'm going into the kitchen. Do you want to come?"

Melissa remained silent as did Windy, as though waiting for Tequila's response. Naturally the snake didn't make a peep, or budge an inch.

Finally Melissa came forward and lifted Tequila with both hands, balancing the reptile carefully. "You can get up now," she told Windy.

"Thanks."

When Windy felt the cool kitchen tiles beneath her feet, she glanced back to see if Tequila had followed. Sure enough, her loyal new friend was right there.

Sky led Windy into his dressing room behind the arena at Rodeo Knights. He had already introduced her to his coworkers, including what he'd called the most important contributors, the quarter horses, palominos and paints that performed to perfection.

As Sky took Windy's hand, she beamed. He had introduced her as his "girlfriend." Not friend or roommate, but girlfriend. Even Charlie had smiled at the affectionate title, sending Windy a playful wink.

Sky closed the door and tossed his hat onto a small counter. The tiny room, cluttered with costumes, sported a plaid recliner, a full-length mirror and an adjoining bathroom. "Do you want to sit down?" he asked.

"Thanks." She smiled and settled into the upholstered chair. "So this is where you change?"

"Yeah." He reached for the top snap on his shirt, pulling it open. "Charlie has a wardrobe lady. She takes care of the clothes, makes sure they're repaired, cleaned, things like that." He touched his shirt—white satin decorated with a rhinestone collar and fringed sleeves. "Fancy, huh?"

She nodded. Besides the shirt, he wore snug denims and a pair of black-and-white leather chaps, equally formfitting. Windy mentally thanked the wardrobe lady. Sky looked good enough to eat. And she wasn't the only female who thought so. She'd heard the feminine catcalls and cheers from the audience during his solo act. "You were incredible out there. Where did you learn to ride like that?"

He removed the shirt. "I don't know. I mean, I don't really remember. Charlie said I was already doing stunts and tricks when he met me. Of course, he says I wasn't very polished, so he figured I was one of those kids who just came by it naturally. Took chances and tried things."

Windy didn't know what the stunts or tricks were called or what style of riding Sky had done, but she'd been more than impressed. He could ride frontward, backward, standing up, kneeling or hanging below the horse's belly. And he'd performed all sorts of rope tricks, some that involved other cast members.

"You must have lived in foster homes where the people had horses."

"Yeah. I have a vague recollection of this big ranch. I think lots of teenagers lived there. Like maybe the owners took in foster kids to help with the chores."

Windy crossed her legs. Tonight she'd chosen a Sante Fe-style skirt, a silk blouse and lizard-skin boots. "I'm getting used to being around horses now. I think I'll be able to ride by myself next time." They had already shared the big gelding several times. "I'm looking forward to going again."

"Yeah, you're doing great. Charlie has a mare he said you could borrow." Sky walked into the rest room and came out, sponging his face with a damp cloth. "She's the horse Melissa rides. I think you'd do fine on her."

"Gingersnap?" Windy asked, recalling the friendly mare at Charlie's house. Charlie and his wife had invited Sky and Windy to dinner last week. She found the parents as charming as their daughter.

"Yeah. Gingersnap. That's the one." He stretched his arms to the ceiling, then leaned against the counter. "I think Missy named her."

Windy leaned forward. "Why don't you have your own horse, Sky?"

"Charlie doesn't mind if I borrow his. And when I'm not working for him, I work as a ranch hand, or a trainer when someone's needin' one. There's always plenty of horses around."

"So you've never owned a horse of your own?"

"No. Tequila's the only companion I've ever had. And sometimes it's tough enough traveling with her. You know, hauling that terrarium around. Sometimes, I just rig some lights for her. It depends on where I'm bunking. Of course, I wouldn't mind having my own place, with my own horses, but, well, you know…"

No, she didn't know. "Maybe it's time for a change, Sky," she said, her voice steadier than the rhythm of her heart. Each week that passed brought them closer to September, closer to his impending departure. "I'm sure Tequila would enjoy having a permanent home. And a man with your skills should have his own ranch, even a mini one." She took a deep breath, reminding herself that he'd referred to her as his girlfriend earlier. "There's plenty of horse property around. Sure, Burbank is too expensive, but the area Charlie lives in is affordable." And Windy had already scanned the newspaper for rentals in that area, preparing for the future. "You and I could lease a place together. Edith wouldn't mind. She wouldn't have trouble finding another tenant."

Sky clawed his fingers through his hair. "Ah, Windy, honey. You know how I feel about California. I just don't belong here."

Windy kept herself focused, determined. If California was the problem, then she'd find a way around it. "We could go someplace else. I could transfer to another university. And there are preschools all over the country." She could make her home anywhere, as long as she was with the man she loved, pursuing the career of her dreams and teaching little children along the way.

Sky came toward her and held out both hands, inviting her to stand. "Let's not get caught up in the future, okay? It's easier on me if we just live day-to-day. No promises, remember?"

She glanced down at their joined hands, willing herself to remain strong. If he left in September, her heart would break, shatter into a million painful pieces. "Okay," she whispered.

Sky brought her hands to his lips and gently grazed her knuckles. "Did you get enough to eat earlier? I can take you out to dinner if you'd like."

She looked into his eyes, praying day-to-day would lead to month-to-month. Year-to-year. "I had the meal they served the audience."

"Yeah, but you don't eat ribs."

"The salad was good. The corn, too. And you know how I love fresh rolls and butter."

He rubbed his nose against hers, in what she thought of as an Eskimo-style kiss. "Don't be sad, Pretty Windy."

"I'm not," her pride responded, as she lifted her chin. "Day-to-day is fine. I was just looking for a little adventure. You know, horses and all that."

"Okay. Good." He turned away and reached for the buckle on his chaps. "I should change."

Windy stood in the tiny dressing room, overwhelmed with the need to keep him close, caress him, press her mouth to his skin and make him shudder. Show him that she loved him. Tell him through her touch that they belonged together.

Now. And forever.

Walking up behind him, she placed her arms around his waist, covered his fingers with her own. "Let me undress you."

Sky turned and dropped his hands, his eyes a blazing shade of blue. "No problem."

Windy released the buckle, then slid her palms over the leather. "How do these…?"

He guided her to the outside seam on the chaps. "They zip."

"You mean unzip," she said, pulling the metal tab down. Divesting him of the fringed garment, she went after his jeans, opening yet another zipper.

She reached into the denims and found his body throbbing from her touch. Pressing her lips to his chest, she kissed each nipple and nudged him toward the chair.

He fell into the recliner and grinned. "Is this where you want me?"

"Yes." She knelt before him and put her mouth against his belly button. He looked too beautiful for words, she thought. A powerful chest and a long, golden torso. Slim hips and denim-clad legs. She opened his jeans farther, exposing the part of him she hungered to taste, tease, arouse.

His grin turned to a groan. "What are you doing?"

"Loving you," she whispered. "The way you love me."

He fisted her hair as though preparing to either pull her away or tug her closer. "Windy, you don't have to…"

Empowered by his struggle, she saw his eyes turn glassy, felt his pulse quicken, his body harden. She pressed her cheek to his thigh, flicked her tongue over him. "I want to."

Sky didn't close his eyes. Instead he watched her, just as she hoped he would. He caressed her face while she loved him, tracing her features, lifting his hips, silently urging her to take more. He tasted of salt and man, of desire and hunger, of a craving neither could seem to control.

"Oh, Windy," he moaned, pulling her up so he could kiss her, slam his tongue into her mouth.

They grappled with unwanted garments, their hands on the other's body, searching for warmth and aroused flesh. While she raked her nails over his chest, he tore the pink lace on her bra and suckled her nipples, his mouth frantic.

Naked except for the lizard boots and a shimmer of gold jewelry, she straddled his waist and teased the tip of his erection, sending a shiver over that smooth, bronzed skin. Somehow, through the blaze of urgency, he growled about needing protection.

Windy dragged him to the floor, spilled the contents of her purse and tore open the foil with her teeth. He entered her where they were, on the carpet, licking and kissing whatever part of her he could reach.

Panting like wild animals, they climaxed, together, on the floor, locked in a primal embrace.

Trembling, Sky fell into her arms. "How am I ever going to live without you?" he asked, his voice raw, breath ragged.

"You're not," she said, holding him possessively against her heart. You're not.

Thirteen

Windy touched her tummy and glanced down at Tequila. The snake was coiled on the bathroom floor beneath a towel, its striped head poking out.

She gathered the remnants from the home pregnancy test and jammed them into the trash. August was nearly over, and since her monthly never arrived, she had begun to suspect the reason.

"I'm pregnant," Windy told her companion, her emotions wavering between shock and pure bliss. "There's a baby in here." Sky's baby.

Windy closed the toilet lid and sat down. Five weeks had passed since her birthday, since the day she'd conceived. It must have happened in the shower the morning after her birthday, the only time Sky had forgotten to use protection. They'd washed each other afterward, and she knew Sky had assumed the gentle cleansing had rinsed his seed away. Naturally, conception hadn't crossed his mind. But then, she hadn't mentioned her missed period, either.

"When should I tell him?" she asked Tequila, suddenly fearful. Although Sky hadn't made plans to leave, he still refused to discuss a future. And September was but a week away.

Windy released a choppy breath, expelling her anxiety. If Sky intended to leave, his bags would be packed by now, and he would have prompted her to find another roommate. September might be a week away, but the man she loved remained, sharing her life and her bed.

"I'll tell him tomorrow," she said, voicing her decision to the snake. Tomorrow was Cowboy Day at the preschool—the perfect day to tell her cowboy lover about his baby. He would visit the school and spend some quality time with her students. And later he'd find out about his own child.

Tequila coiled herself into a tighter ball, and Windy smiled. "Oh, he's going to be a little scared when I tell him, but what expectant parent isn't?" She cradled her tummy and closed her eyes, picturing Sky with their baby. Oh, yes, she could see the tiny life cuddled against his broad chest, cooing soft baby sounds and dreaming sweet baby dreams.

Windy opened her eyes, her heart brimming with motherhood. "I'll be patient with Sky, give him time to adjust." She leaned forward to stroke Tequila's head. "But don't worry," she assured the animal as much as herself, "once the initial shock wears off, he'll be as happy as I am."

Deep down, she thought, Sky adored children, secretly longed to have his own. All the signs were there: his relationship with Melissa, his fears about fatherhood. She remembered on their first date Sky had worried aloud about his parental skills. Why would a man be concerned about being a good father if he didn't want children?

She stood in front of the mirror and studied her reflection. Her hair wasn't so bad, she decided. Sky loved her rebellious curls, and he'd be thrilled to have a daughter with long golden waves, just as she'd be proud to have a blue-eyed, black-haired son.

She cocked her head, touched her lips in remembrance, tasting Sky's last kiss. *He loves me. Skyler loves me.*

He hadn't said so, not out loud, but she felt it in his touch, saw it in his smile whenever they made love. And soon he would know their loving had created a child, a tiny life growing in her womb.

A soft knock sounded on the door. "Windy, honey?"

Oh, my God.

"Sky?" she croaked, staring at the trash can, at the discarded pregnancy kit crunched on top. "How long have you been home?"

"A little while," he answered through the closed door. "I can't find Tequila. Is she with you?"

"Yes." She shot the snake a warning look, then almost laughed at her nervousness. Tequila couldn't talk. A reptile didn't need to be reprimanded about keeping secrets. "We're cleaning the bathroom."

Windy heard Sky chuckle, hoping he wouldn't try the door. "That snake follows you around like a puppy," he said. "You spoil her rotten."

Rather than respond, she scrambled for the trash and tied the bag, hiding the incriminating evidence. "Tomorrow," she whispered. Tomorrow she would tell Sky about their baby.

Sky walked through the narrow doorway, wishing he could turn tail and run. Career Week at the preschool was in full swing, and today was Cowboy Day. He didn't like the idea of having to interact with a bunch of tots. Performing in an arena was different. This gig required him to look the audience straight in the eye, be himself, rather than hide behind fancy duds and a rope.

He found room three and stood in the hallway, listening to the activity and happy chatter. Damning himself for being conned, he opened the door and stepped inside.

"The cowboy's here!" one of the children squealed, his tiny voice rising a decibel above the noisy room.

Anonymity wasn't possible, Sky realized. Not when he

stood over six feet and wore black boots and a Stetson to match. He scanned the tables where the children sat, searching for Windy.

She found him at the same moment. Their eyes met, and she smiled. He held on to her stare like a lifeline, praying he wouldn't disappoint her or the sea of little faces gazing up at him.

She came toward him and reached for his hand, gave it an encouraging squeeze. "This is my friend Sky," she told her students. "He's going to visit with us today. But first I'll collect your pictures. We'll have time to finish them later." She released Sky's hand and instructed the class to say a collective hello.

After the kids greeted him, he nodded and moved closer to observe their artwork. Apparently Windy had provided them with a picture of a pony. Some kids, he mused, had colored the animal blue or green. One happy little boy had decorated his with polka dots.

"Looks like an Appaloosa," Sky told the child. "They have spots."

The freckle-faced kid flashed a gap-toothed grin. "You a real cowboy?"

He nodded. "Yep."

"You kinda look like an Indian," another boy remarked.

Sky shifted his booted feet. "I'm an Indian who works as a cowboy."

"You got boo eyes," a blond-haired girl said. "So do I."

Sky almost touched the top of her pig-tailed head. No one had ever called his eyes boo before.

Windy managed to collect the artwork and keep the children in their seats. Sky marveled at her patience and nourishing manner. Adoration shone on those young faces as they gazed up at her. It made him feel like a heel, being there, pretending to be worthy of her affection.

Windy wrangled the group into a semicircle on the carpet so they could learn from their guest. At that dawning moment, Sky wished Charlie or some other cowboy had agreed to do this. Some of the kids wiggled and giggled, while others sat wide-eyed, waiting for him to speak.

Windy had suggested a simple explanation of his profession so the children could decipher movie heroes from the real thing. Sky lowered himself to the ground and looked to her for support. Thankfully, she took charge.

"Does anyone know how cowboys got their name?" she asked.

The kids started spouting answers, but Windy reminded them to raise their hands. The first hand that shot up belonged to the freckle-faced boy who'd created the polka-dotted pony.

"Patrick?" she said.

"They wear cowboy hats," the boy responded.

Cute kid, Sky thought, animated and friendly. "That's right…um…Patrick, they do," Sky said, doing his best to speak correctly, rather than use slang words the way he usually did. "But the first cowboys were children, boys in Texas who helped with the family ranch and herded cattle when their fathers and older brothers went off to war. So you see, someone decided to call the boys who roped cows—cowboys."

"Did they milk the cows?" one of the girls quickly asked, raising her hand after the fact.

"No," Sky answered. "They used this type of cattle for meat, not milk."

"Did the cows have babies?" the girl persisted.

Uh-oh. Sky prayed he wouldn't have to explain the mating ritual between a bull and a cow to a bunch of four-year-olds. "Sometimes," he said, hoping that would suffice. He made a mental note not to use the word steer, fearing some curious kid would ask him what it meant. Castration wasn't part of the cowboy lesson he intended to share.

"I can moo like a cow," the same girl remarked.

"Me, too," another little voice chirped.

The conversation strayed to farm animals and the sounds they made. Sky relaxed as the kids conversed with Windy. They called her Miss Windy, he noticed, a ladylike name for a sweet and proper woman.

"Tell the kids about how many different types of cowboys there are," Windy coaxed, as Patrick moved closer to Sky.

Sky nodded and drew his knees up, realizing the freckle-faced boy was mimicking his actions. He winked at the kid and told the group about modern-day ranchers and rodeo cowboys, and then about his own job and the trick riding and roping he did.

It amazed him that the children were so attentive, and that they hung on his every word. Windy, too. He'd glance up to catch her gazing at him, a dreamy smile on her lips. He found himself smiling back, wishing he could stay with her. Windy had suggested they live together permanently, find a piece of horse property to share. Of course, that would never do. He wasn't the right man for Pretty Windy. He'd already mapped his future by screwing up his past. Skyler, the drifter, would be leaving in September, going wherever the autumn winds blew.

Windy took over the lesson and read from a children's book about horses, delighting a rambunctious, yet captive, audience. Sky watched her, thinking how dedicated she was, how soft and pretty. Although her dress had acquired a few wrinkles since she'd left home and her pale canvas shoes were splattered with what looked like grape juice, a smile shone in her eyes. The kind of smile that could make a man want. And want. And want.

Sky shook his head. Quit wanting, damn it. And quit wishing for what could never be. Windy was better off without him. It didn't matter that—

That what? he asked himself, his mouth suddenly dry. That he cared about her? Loved her? Oh, dear God. He loved her. Him. The man who ran from commitment.

Sky looked down at his boots, at the worn heels and scuffed leather tops. Did it matter? Love wasn't the cure-all movies and books made it out to be. It wouldn't guarantee happily-ever-after or change who he was or what he'd done. He had still committed an unforgivable sin, and loving Windy wouldn't ease his conscience. If anything, the feeling only intensified his self-loathing.

When the story ended, Sky rose to his feet and watched Windy guide her students back to the tables, the kids quacking around her like dependent little ducklings.

She looked back and smiled, sending his aching heart askew. He returned the smile, hoping to conceal the violent pounding in his chest. Should he leave Windy without confessing his sin? No, he thought. She'd get over him easier if she knew the truth. Get over him? Hell, she'd hate him.

"Mr. Sky?"

He glanced down to see Patrick peering up at him. He touched the boy's shoulder. "What is it, son?"

"Will you help me color my apple-oosa?"

"Sure."

The children who had already finished their pictures were given puzzles to complete. Sky sat between Patrick and another boy and watched the kids color. Soon he found himself lost in the waxy smell of crayons and sound of incessant chatter.

Windy made her way around the tables, stopping to praise each child. "Very nice, Patrick. Your horse is quite colorful."

The boy beamed. "It's an apple-oosa. Mr. Sky said so."

Windy sent Sky a smile so loving, his heart nearly broke. What she wanted, he realized, was a lifetime with him, right down to their own children. When she moved on to the next table, he lifted a crayon from the box, his mood melancholy. Lonely and sad.

"Did you like to draw when you was a kid?" Patrick asked.

"Yeah," Sky answered automatically, suddenly remembering himself as a boy, a sad and lonely child, sitting in a classroom filled with unfamiliar faces. "I used to draw cars and trucks." And he used to fight back his tears every morning, wishing his parents hadn't gone to Heaven. Sky had hated being the new kid at school, almost as much as he'd hated that big white house where the social worker had taken him to live.

Stunned by the jolt of memory, he glanced out the window and caught sight of the empty playground. That house, the one he'd hated, had a swing set and a metal slide out back. His first foster home, he realized. He could see it clearly in his mind, right down to the freshly painted porch.

"I lived in a big white house," he said out loud, "in Arrow Hill, Oklahoma." Oklahoma. Dear God. He was born in Oklahoma.

"Our house is yellow," Patrick offered, unaware of Sky's trembling hands. "And we live in Burbank, California. I even know my whole address. Did you know your address when you was a kid? My mom says kids is smarter these days."

"Yeah, I knew." Sky touched a strand of the child's reddish-brown hair, reciting the address of that big white house as though he'd never forgotten it. "I lived at 618 Shepard Lane." And I used to hold Jesse at night and think about running away. Of course he hadn't run away until years later. And by then, he was living in another foster home, but he couldn't remember that address, or even what the place looked like. He'd lived in so many different foster homes.

"Do you have a teddy bear?" Sky asked Patrick, wondering why Jesse was still so damn important to him.

"Naw. I'm too big for them kind of toys. I can write already. Miss Windy showed us how. See?" The boy slid his paper toward Sky, displaying a set of crooked letters. "That's my name. Could you do that when you was four?"

"I don't know." Sky sat for a moment, staring at Patrick's picture. I should leave tonight, he told himself. Go to that house in Oklahoma. Try to remember my name, find my son and be the father I should have been.

Windy entered the house, silently reexamining the events of her day. Much to her disappointment, Sky had left the preschool before lunch, apparently feeling the need to escape. Oh, he had winked and smiled at the kids on his way out, even knelt to hug those who had given him their artwork, but Windy had seen the confusion in his eyes.

Don't worry, she told herself. So Sky had seemed perplexed. That wasn't necessarily a bad thing. It was possible the kids had triggered an emotion he hadn't expected to feel—a startling urge to settle down. And an urge like that would bewilder a man who had fashioned himself a drifter.

Windy touched her tummy. Was that the answer? Had Sky just discovered his need for a wife? A family? A lifetime of commitment?

Please, God, let it be so.

She closed her eyes. That had to be the explanation for Sky's odd behavior. It just had to be. She loved him too much to lose him, to accept any other reason.

Windy opened her eyes. All right, it was time to react, to find Sky and tell him about their baby. What should she do first? Ask him why he had left the preschool early, or get right to her news?

Play it by ear, she decided, gauge his mood, study the expression in his eyes, try to read the sentiment in his heart. If Sky struggled too deeply with the confusion he'd felt earlier, then she'd wait to tell him about their child. He might need some time to adjust to his newfound feelings.

After Windy passed Tequila's cage, she peered into an empty kitchen. Sky must be in his room. Although he didn't sleep in his own room, he spent quiet time there, often immersed in a book. Windy had come to realize Sky's misuse of the English language was a tough-guy habit he'd picked up as a youth and in no way affected his reading skills. He carried a stack of library cards in his wallet as numerous and well used as Windy's credit cards.

She stepped into the kitchen. So Sky was probably reading, relaxing on his bed with a library book. She twisted a strand of her hair, twining it around her finger. Maybe this was a bad time to disturb him. Maybe he wanted to be alone. Maybe…

Windy opened a cabinet and admonished herself. Maybe she had better get her nerves in check because regardless of what Sky was doing, it wasn't as important as their future. She reached for a glass and filled it with water, hoping the cool liquid would help.

Several sips later she placed the glass in the sink and headed down the hall. Dang it. Why the apprehension, the anxiety? Deep down she knew Sky loved her. And once he accepted loving her, he'd accept the idea of having a baby, too.

Windy paused at Sky's bedroom door, contemplated knocking, then quickly dismissed the idea. Sky had left the door slightly ajar, which meant he welcomed her company. And why wouldn't he? They had spent many a lazy afternoon snuggling in his bed, drinking iced tea and eating sugar cookies, kissing, laughing and loving the day away.

Relishing those memories, she pushed open the door. Immediately her gaze connected with several pairs of blue jeans strewn across the bed. Next to the rumpled denim sat a half-filled duffel bag.

"Sky?"

He stood at the closet, a handful of shirts folded over his arm.

"What are you doing?"

He turned toward her, then froze, his posture stiff, unnatural. "Packing."

Everything, including her heart, went still. "Why?"

He flinched as though her question had pierced his chest, as though the answer had become lodged in his throat.

Windy brought her arms around her waist, cradling the tiny life there. She didn't need to hear the answer. The haunting look in his eyes said it all.

God help her. The man she loved, the father of her baby, was leaving.

For good.

Fourteen

Sky avoided Windy's gaze, feeling like the worst kind of bastard. He knew she struggled to look brave and fight back her tears, but her soft brown eyes reminded him of a gentle doe about to be gunned down. And damn it, he was the guy holding the rifle.

But remember, once she finds out you walked out on an innocent child, she'll hate you. She'll want you out of her life.

"I'm going to Oklahoma." He lowered the shirts and told her about his memory flashes at the preschool. "My flight leaves around ten. I was gonna drive, but when I came home to service my truck, I noticed it was leaking oil." He'd spent hours trying to fix the leak, but had finally given up. "I'll deal with the repairs when I get back."

Windy moved toward the bed, sat down. "You're coming back?" she asked, her voice edged with hope.

Sky forced himself to look at her. "Yeah, but I'll be movin' on again." He intended to stay in Oklahoma for a few days, find a place to bunk, then return to California for Tequila and his truck. He could have postponed the trip and repaired his truck first, but had decided to fly instead; he was much too impatient to see his hometown. "You knew I planned on leaving in September. And now I've got a place to go." He pictured the white house on Shepard Street. "The first thing I'm gonna do is stop by my old foster home, see if it triggers more memories."

She pitched forward a little, holding her stomach as though it suddenly ached. "That was a long time ago, Sky. The house might be gone by now."

"Yeah, I know." He realized there could be a shopping center in its place, or fancy new condominiums. "But I've got to go there, anyway. It's all I have."

She glanced down at her trembling hands. "You have me."

Not for long, he thought, already missing her. He had wanted to be packed by the time she got home, but had spent too much time trying to fix his truck, and now she was there, watching him through misty eyes. He had to finish packing, yet he couldn't seem to find the strength to move.

"When I get back, I'll give Edith some extra money so you don't have to worry about finding a roommate for a while." He wanted to take care of her somehow, even if he was gone. "Take your time and find a nice girl to share this place with," he said, struggling to smile. "Don't let some wise-crackin' cowboy move in."

The wounded look in her eyes said she didn't want to find another roommate, and the only cowboy she wanted to live with was the one shredding her heart. "I love you," she whispered.

Sky moved toward her, dropped his shirts onto the bed. He loved her, too, even though he had no right to.

"No. You don't really know who I am. If you did, you wouldn't love me."

"You're wrong. And I've told you that before. You're a good person, and that's part of why I fell in love with you." Before he could protest, she latched on to both of his hands and continued, "You risked your own life to save Edith's, and

you let Hank give you a black eye so Lucy could get away.''
She tightened her grip when he tried to pull away, determined
to finish her speech. ''And even though you won't admit it,
you have a natural way with children. My students wanted to
know when you were coming back. They adored you, Sky.''

''Oh, God.'' This time he managed to pull away, free himself from her desperate hold. ''I have a son, Windy.''

She sat silent for a long moment, just staring up at him, her
eyes filled with question, worry. Confusion and pain. Clearly,
she wondered if the existence of his child meant there was
another woman in his life. ''How old is he?'' she asked finally.

He began stuffing his jeans into the duffel bag, needing
something to do. ''He was, I don't know, about two when I
left. This happened a long time ago, Windy. When I was a
teenager.''

''Did you just remember him today?''

Sky's voice quivered. ''No. I've known about him for a
while.''

She placed a shaky hand against her chest, against the buttons on her dress. She still wore the same clothes from earlier,
right down to the juice-stained shoes. ''You knew you had a
son all this time and you didn't tell me?''

He expelled a heavy breath. ''I'm sorry. I hadn't planned
on getting involved with you. And I'm used to keeping my
personal life to myself. Besides, do you know how hard it is
for me to admit what I've done? I walked out on my own kid.
I couldn't handle being a dad, so I split.'' He shoved his shirts
into the bag and continued, ''I'm not sure about the details.
Some of it's pretty vague, but I figure besides the threat of
being sent to reform school, that little boy was the reason I
ran away. Let's face it, I was a hellion. Raising a kid would
have cramped my style.''

Windy's tone, as well as her jerky movements, bordered on
panic. ''You wouldn't have done something like that. You
must be confusing your memories somehow.'' She clutched
her tummy. ''Why would you have deserted your own son,

then risked your life to save Edith, a virtual stranger on the street corner? That doesn't make sense.''

"Damn it, Windy. Don't make excuses for me. I know what I did.'' And maybe he'd put himself in front of that car on purpose. Maybe his conscience had gotten to him.

She gazed up at the ceiling as though searching for answers she could live with. "If your son was two when you left, that means you would have been fifteen, maybe even fourteen when he was conceived. That's awfully young, Sky. You must be confusing him with someone else's child.''

"Oh, Windy,'' he mumbled, wishing she would just accept what he'd done. "You know as well as I do that plenty of fourteen- and fifteen-year-old boys are capable of fathering a child.''

"What's your son's name?'' she asked, apparently hell-bent on challenging his memory.

"I don't remember.'' He sent her a determined look. "But I know he has black hair and light-gray eyes.''

She held his stare, clearly struggling with her heart. A woman in love, defying the inevitable, denying the truth. "Who's the boy's mother?''

A tight, cynical laugh barked from his chest. "Hell, I don't know. I don't remember her at all. I don't even recall the day I left my son. I just know I did.'' As an image of the child came to mind, he glanced away from Windy, from the confusion in her eyes. "I do remember apologizing to him, though. Telling him some bull about not being old enough to take care of him. But all he did was cry.''

She heaved a sigh, a breath of what sounded like more false hope. "Do you hear what you're saying? You didn't want to leave him, but you had to for some reason.'' She reached out and held his hand once again. "You remember the boy, at least for the first two years of his life, which means you were involved in his care.'' She tightened her grip, forcing him to meet her gaze. "Don't you see, Sky? You must have given him up for adoption.''

Adoption? Sky took a step back, freeing his hand. His memories were nothing but scattered images, bits and pieces of a broken puzzle. But they didn't include adoption.

"All I know is that I split. Walked out on someone who wanted to keep me."

Windy hugged herself. "And if you leave in September, you'll be doing it again."

The pain, the sadness in her eyes made him want to hold her. Instead, he stepped back even farther. He had to end their relationship. Now. She was supposed to hate him for abandoning his child, not pretend he'd been some noble teen who'd given the boy up for adoption. "We don't belong together, Windy."

"You're wrong. You aren't the type of person who could have deliberately walked away from his own child, even as a teenager. Your memories are failing you somehow."

Damn it. He had to make her realize he was no good, that she deserved better. "You want me to be someone I'm not. You want marriage and kids, but that's not me. Sure, I plan on finding my son, but all I can do at this point is help him out financially." Sky decided not to tell her that he intended to be the father he should have been, even if it took the rest of his life. That would only reinforce Windy's misguided belief in him.

"I don't want any more kids," he said, knowing the lie would sever Windy's feelings for him. Although he'd taken precautions to prevent pregnancy, a part of him wanted the chance to father another child. A child with Windy. But how could he bring another life into the world without total acceptance from the son he'd left behind? And asking Windy to wait wouldn't be fair. "Why do you think I've been so careful about using protection? I didn't want to take the risk of getting you pregnant."

She flinched as though she'd been stabbed, but he remained where he stood, hating himself for wounding her. For allowing her to fall in love with him. And damn it, for falling in love himself.

Windy felt a gasp of air rush painfully from her lungs. Oh,

God, what should she do? Sky didn't want children, yet she carried his babe in her womb. "There was that one time we forgot to use protection," she said, struggling to keep herself from breaking down.

"Yeah, but it didn't happen, so there's nothing to worry about."

Nothing to worry about. She was pregnant and the man she loved was leaving, flying to Oklahoma, while her bruised and battered heart still longed for him. He didn't want children—not even with her.

Sky rolled up his shirtsleeves and reached for the duffel bag, exposing a gash on his arm.

"What happened?" she asked instinctively.

He turned his wrist and studied his arm. "I cut it when I was trying to fix my truck. It's no big deal."

"You should let me put some antiseptic on it," she heard herself say. "And a bandage, too." Lord help her, but she needed to touch him, breathe his scent, imprint the texture of his skin into her mind.

"Okay." He placed his luggage on the floor. "I suppose it could get infected. And I have a few minutes."

Windy's legs carried her numbly to the bathroom and back. Sky sat beside her on the bed while she opened the first-aid kit. She touched him gently, nursing his injury with care. He was, and would always be, the man she loved. The father of her child.

"Pretty Windy." He pleaded her name with apology, and their eyes met. The long, lingering gaze caused her tears to flow. One by one they dropped onto her cheeks, clouding her vision before they fell. Sky reached for her and pressed her head against his chest, stroking her hair with his bandaged arm.

Windy buried her face in his shirt and cried soundlessly. This is where I belong, she thought, in his arms.

Tell him, her mind implored. Tell him about the baby. He had a right to know. And regardless of what Sky had said about his other child, Windy didn't believe he had abandoned the boy purposely. If she told Sky about their baby, he'd stay. He would remain with her out of honor and duty.

"Sky—" she lifted her head "—I..." Honor and duty? Was that what she wanted? "I'm sorry, I didn't mean to cry." She worked free from his embrace and dried her tears with the palm of her hand. She wouldn't belittle herself by trying to keep a man who didn't want to stay. He made the choice to leave and she would let him. From that moment on, the baby she carried would be hers. Hers alone.

"I'm fine now," she said, lifting her chin defiantly.

He stood, backed away. He wore jeans and the dusty black boots he favored, his hair banded into a tight ponytail. "I wonder if your son looks like you," she said. "If he's as tall and dark." She didn't believe there was a child at first, but Sky seemed so sure.

Sky shrugged. "He might be eighteen by now. A man in his own right."

Windy nodded and gazed at Sky, remembering the intimacy they had once shared. He had been her best friend, her lover. Now it seemed as though he was neither.

"I'll be back in a few days," he said. "You don't mind taking care of Tequila while I'm gone, do you?"

"No, not at all." Windy had come to think of the snake as her spirit animal as well. "She's no trouble."

He managed a smile. "You've come a long way in three months, Pretty Windy."

"You'd better go." She fought another flood of tears and looked away, knowing she had already lost the man she loved. He'd be back, but not to stay. Their summer fling had left her pregnant and alone. An unwed mother with a broken heart.

The following afternoon Sky stood in front of the house on Shepard street, thinking it looked a bit smaller than he remembered and far less intimidating. But then, he was no longer a frightened child, fresh with grief from the loss of his parents.

The tree-lined street lent the neighborhood a suburban charm, as did manicured lawns and carefully tended flower beds. He could hear the murmur of bees buzzing through the quiet, sweltering Oklahoma air.

With sweat beading his brow, he took another step toward the porch, then stopped, struggling to remember his name.

Sky…

Skyler…

Damn it. Why couldn't he recall something as important as his last name? The name that had belonged to his father.

Suddenly an image flashed through Sky's mind—a tall, broad-shouldered man with copper skin and a thick, black ponytail. My dad. My strong, protective dad.

Immediately a woman's image followed, and he knew the blond-haired, blue-eyed beauty was his mother. She had been young and vibrant, gentle and sweet. And she had died with her husband on a humid summer night when another vehicle collided with their truck.

Sky approached the porch and sat on the first step, his head between his hands. All the grief, the awful, lonely pain came gushing back like an icy river flowing through his veins. The warmth and comfort he had known as a child had died in that battered old pickup. And soon after, a social worker had taken him to Shepard Street, leaving him, teddy bear in hand, at someone else's home.

"What are you doing on my property?" an angry female voice asked.

Startled, Sky turned to gaze up at the woman at her front door, wedged in the small opening she had allowed.

"I'm sorry. I…" He stood and gripped the porch rail. "I used to live here."

She cocked her head. "You must be mistaken. I've owned this house for over thirty-five years, and no one but me and mine have lived here."

"It was a long time ago." He skimmed his fingers over the painted wood rail. "But I'm certain it was this house. I was a foster chi—"

"Oh, my," she said, releasing her hold on the door.

Sky remained on the bottom step as she approached. She

was a stern-looking Native American woman with short, graying hair and a stout, stocky body. She didn't seem familiar, yet he knew she must have been his first foster mother.

"Take those sunglasses off," she ordered from her perch above him.

He removed them and stood in the patch of sunlight that crossed the steps.

A smile softened the lines around her mouth. "Blue as ever." She gestured for him to come closer, apparently certain of his identity.

He slipped the sunglasses into his pocket and climbed onto the porch. "I'm sorry but I don't remember your name."

"Maggie. Maggie Redbow." She sat down in a white wicker chair and invited him to do the same. "And you're little Sky, all grown up. You were the only foster child we ever had. You stayed here for about a year. Our own kids never really got used to the idea of another child living with us, so we realized being foster parents wasn't going to work."

A sea of questions flooded his mind, but before he could pose even one, Maggie spoke again.

"You know, Jesse was here. Eleven, maybe twelve years ago. He found you, didn't he? That boy had been searching everywhere."

Jesse? Sky rubbed his temples. The only Jesse he remembered was a worn-out teddy bear.

He turned to Maggie. "My son was here?"

"Goodness, no. I don't know anything about your son. I was talking about your brother."

Immediately Sky's heart knocked against his chest, sending images surging through his brain. The gray-eyed boy crying as a social worker carried him away. Sky, as a child himself, rubbing his own teary eyes.

Pain. Fear. Loneliness. The loss of his…brother? Yes. Oh, God, yes. Sweet, trusting two-year-old Jesse.

"They separated us," he said, struggling to still his quaking hands. "Jesse went to a different foster home." Sky gazed at Maggie Redbow and realized, with a startling mix of relief and regret, that he had no son. The boy in his nightmare was his baby brother. And Sky hadn't been a teenager when he'd lost Jesse. He'd been a child himself, an orphaned six-year-old. "But when the social worker took him away, she had forgotten about his teddy bear."

Maggie only nodded. "Like I said, your brother was here."

Sky's breath hitched as another memory invaded his mind. Adoption… Windy had said something about adoption. That was it, the reason he had lost touch with Jesse. Not long after he and Jesse were separated, he'd asked the social worker about seeing his brother. But he'd been told the other child was in the process of being adopted, so visiting Jesse wasn't possible. Sky had cried that day, believing he had lost his baby brother forever.

"Did he leave an address or a number where he could be reached?"

"No, but he said he'd be back someday. Of course, he hasn't been. At least not that I know of."

"What was he like?"

Maggie gazed up at the porch roof, then back at Sky. "He looked similar to you, but he was leaner, and his eyes were sort of a silvery color. He was only eighteen then, so I would imagine he's changed quite a bit. He's probably filled out the way men do."

"What about his personality? Did he seem happy? Was he talkative, quiet?"

She folded her hands on her lap. "Quiet, I suppose. It was so long ago, and it was such a brief visit. He seemed determined to find you, though. He'd already been to all of your other foster homes."

Sky closed his eyes. Oh, Jesse, little brother, where are you now?

Windy was right, he thought. The amnesia had confused him, jumbled fact and fiction in his mind. Somehow Sky had transposed his scattered memories of Jesse with the struggle from his teenage years, making him think they were connected.

I didn't abandon a child. Jesse had been taken from him, and he'd kept his brother's teddy bear all those years, even though he couldn't recall its importance.

Sky smiled. Windy would help him find Jesse. She'd…

The smile faded. How could he expect Windy to help him after the hurtful things he'd said to her? He'd never even told her that he loved her. Yet all along she'd believed in him, loved him with an unconditional acceptance most men could only dream about.

He had to go back to California and apologize to Windy, beg her forgiveness. And he'd do it tonight. He couldn't lose Pretty Windy. Not now. Not ever. How could he have left her, alone and crying?

Sky stood. "Maggie, I know this is going to sound like an odd question. But, what was my name when the social worker first brought me here? You know, my legal name?" Sky intended to propose to Windy, but he couldn't very well offer her his name if he didn't know what it was.

"Skyler Michael Hawk," she answered. "At least that's what I was told."

Skyler Michael Hawk. He gazed out at the trees that lined the walkway. Suddenly the name felt as familiar as his own heartbeat.

Hawk. Just like the bird, the messenger in his dreams. Sky tested his brother's name in his mind. Jesse Hawk. Jesse Aaron Hawk. His beautiful baby brother, the boy his heart had never forgotten. "If it's okay, I'd like to leave my number with you in case Jesse ever comes back."

"Certainly." Maggie slipped into the house and returned with a small leather address book. Sky wrote Windy's number, hoping, praying she'd take him back.

Late that evening Sky arrived in California, only to find Windy missing. Tequila slept in Windy's bed, but the lady was nowhere to be found.

"Damn," he cursed nervously. "Where could she be?" It was after midnight on a weekday. Windy should have been home, snuggled between the sheets, her wild mane fanned across a pillow.

Uncertain of what do to, he reached for the phone, preparing to call Edith. But as he lifted the receiver, he noticed the blinking light on Windy's answering machine, signaling a message.

He pushed the play button and listened.

"Umm…Windy," an anxious voice said, "I don't know if you remember me, but my name is Lucy. You said I could call if I ever needed—"

God, no. Sky stared at the machine, his heart clenching with an unbearable ache. Apparently Windy had intercepted the call, which meant she was with Lucy somewhere. And if Lucy was in trouble, then so was Windy, because, Sky knew, the two of them didn't stand a chance in hell against Lucy's abusive husband.

Windy had never been so exhausted in her life, or so weak. Her limbs wobbled as she walked. Dizziness, she knew, was common in the early stages of pregnancy, but she had never expected fainting spells to happen to her. Of course, it had been a long night, filled with emotion. She unlocked the front door, stepped inside and found herself blasted with a frantic, masculine curse.

"Damn it. Do you know what time it is? I've been worried sick."

Immediately her legs gained consistency. She wouldn't dare collapse in front of Sky. And what was he doing back so soon, anyway? He'd only been gone one night, and dang it, she had just begun to put his features out of her mind. Forced herself to forget that determined jaw and those sparkling blue eyes. But now he was there—tempting her nostrils with his woodsy cologne.

Windy lifted her chin. Her pride couldn't take much more. The man had walked out on her. "Since when do I have to answer to you?"

"Since you decided to go off on your own and play Wonder Woman. Do you know how scared I was when I heard that message on your answering machine?'' He pulled a hand through his already tousled hair. "You had no business trying to save the day. You should have called the police. They would have helped Lucy.''

Giving in to her exhaustion, Windy lowered herself onto the couch. The tiny baby in her womb deserved a strong, healthy mother. "Lucy needed me.'' And being needed had felt good. Taking Lucy and her children to the women's shelter had warmed the shattered pieces of Windy's heart.

Sky sat on the end of the coffee table, too close for comfort. "So the fact that Lucy has an abusive husband didn't concern you?''

"Hank is in jail. He was arrested for drunk driving. It was his second DUI, so Lucy knew he'd be detained for a while.''

Clearly Sky wasn't satisfied. "Hank has that psycho brother, you know.''

"Jimmy's a truck driver. He was on the road.'' Windy met his gaze, refusing to apologize for helping someone in need. "Lucy wasn't in any danger, and neither was I. She realized this was the perfect opportunity to get away, so she called me.''

"Oh.'' His expression softened. "Well, I was worried, ya know. Edith wasn't home, either, and that just upset me more. I've been pacing all night.''

"Edith waited for us at the shelter.'' She glanced away, wishing she didn't love him so desperately. "Everything's fine now, so feel free to move on when you're ready.''

"Is that what you want, Pretty Windy? For me to go?''

She forced herself to look at him. "It's what you wanted. You're the one who left, remember?''

"Yeah, I remember.'' He heaved a loud sigh, and she realized he was as emotionally spent as she. "You were right about my son, Windy. He doesn't exist. The little boy I kept dreaming about was my brother.''

Windy's heart lunged to her throat. So Sky didn't have a child. She touched her tummy. At least not one he knew about. "You have a younger brother?''

"Yeah." He smiled. "His name's Jesse. And that teddy bear belonged to him."

Instinctively she reached for Sky's hand. "So you met him?"

His smile faded. "No, but my foster mother said he'd been looking for me. Of course, that was about eleven years ago." He slid his fingers between hers and settled himself beside her. "My parents died when I was six and Jesse was two. We were separated and taken to different foster homes. That's how I ended up with Jesse's teddy bear. The social worker accidentally left it behind."

He brought their linked hands to his cheek and closed his eyes, his expression sad. "God, all those dreams. All those nights of hearing Jesse cry." He opened his eyes and lowered their hands, slipping his fingers from hers. "I have to find him. But I don't know where to start. Oklahoma's a big state, and he might not even be there anymore."

Windy took a deep breath. Beautiful Sky. Beautiful orphaned Sky. She tried to picture Jesse, wondering if the brothers looked alike. Did they share the same ebony hair and dimpled smile? The same copper skin and long fluid body?

Windy touched her stomach. Would her baby inherit those features, too? "You should contact one of those search organizations. You know, the kind that help family members find each other. All you have to do is leave Jesse's name. And yours." She paused as her heart skipped an anxious beat. "Oh, my God, Sky, did you find out what your last name is?"

"Hawk," he answered softly. "Just like the birds we've been seeing."

Windy's eyes began to mist. "Your messengers."

"Yeah. But I'm not sure if Hawk is still Jesse's last name. I think he was adopted, at least that's what I remember the social worker telling me when I asked to see him." He pulled his hands through his hair. "Do you think you could help me find him, Windy?"

"Of course," she said, as their eyes met. "I'll always be here if you need me." She could never turn away from Sky.

If friendship was all he could offer, then she would raise his child and be his friend, even though she would always long for more. "We can start looking for Jesse right away. I know how important this is to you."

He placed his finger against her lips and traced their shape, slowly. Gently. "Thank you. Just knowing that you'll be here, that I can count on you…"

She savored the stolen moment of intimacy, the longing and the need. "You can, Sky. Always."

"Always?" He slid his finger from her lips to her cheek, skimming lightly. A soft, yet rough, touch. Calloused and masculine. "Does that mean you still love me?"

She caught her breath. She'd love him until her dying day. "Yes."

His eyes, the bright-blue eyes she adored, turned watery. "I love you, too, Pretty Windy."

She gripped the couch for support. Suddenly her limbs felt molten. She had thought he'd loved her before, but he'd walked away. "You don't want children," she heard herself say. She was carrying his baby, and he didn't want children. Love couldn't mend that. Could it?

He sighed. "That's not true. Of course, I'm grateful that I didn't abandon anyone, but a part of me is actually mourning the loss of not having a child. I'd kind of gotten used to the idea of being a father." He reached for her hand. Her shaky hand. "I said a lot of things I didn't mean. I came back because I love you. And if you're able to forgive me, I'd like to stay. I had no right to hurt you like that, but I was trying to set you free so you could go on with your life." He paused for what sounded like an anxious breath. "But damn it, I don't want to set you free. I want you to be my wife, the mother of my children. And we can stay in California if you want to. Wherever you are is home to me. I know that now."

He searched her face. "So will you marry me, Pretty Windy? Sleep with me every night and make lots of babies?"

She blinked through a glaze of tears. He wanted a wife. Children. A lifetime of love and commitment. She brought his hand to her tummy. "Of course I'll marry you, but we already made a baby. You're going to be a father in the spring."

His hand froze. "Oh, God. Really?" He studied her intently, his fingers still splayed tenderly across her stomach. "How long have you known? Why didn't you tell me?"

She placed her hand over his, cradling their baby. "I was going to tell you before you left, but then you said you didn't want children, and I—"

He gathered her into his arms and rocked gently, his husky voice raspier than usual. "I'm such a jerk. I should have never said that to you. God, what you must have been going through." He nuzzled her neck, burying his face in her hair. "I'm so sorry. I don't know what made me think that I could survive without you."

She held him close, tight against her heart. "Everything is okay now, Sky. We're going to be fine. All of us."

He kissed her then. A slow, mesmerizing kiss. He was crying, too, she realized, those gorgeous blue eyes damp with apology.

"I love you," he whispered. "You and our baby."

She loved him, too, this tall, cowboy drifter who invaded every beat of her heart, every breath she took. She moved his hand to the buttons on her blouse, inviting him to undress her. She needed to feel his body against hers, be touched by the man she loved. And she needed to caress him, run her fingers over the planes and angles that formed his staggering beauty. Skyler Hawk belonged to her now—to her and the tiny life their love had created.

Epilogue

Sky steered the rental car down the graveled driveway. It was a beautiful day in Oklahoma, early spring and unseasonably warm. Trees lined the walk, and a bed of daffodils sprouted from the soil, splashing color along the front of the house. The house itself, woodsy and rustic, boasted paned windows and a large, inviting porch. Sky could imagine rocking his baby to sleep on that porch, humming lullabies while the infant's eyelids fluttered, the tiny body snug against his own.

He parked the car and smiled at his wife. Windy was heavy with child, the babe in her womb growing daily. She wore pregnancy well, glowing, as they say, her skin dewy, her hair as vibrant as the sun.

"Are you nervous?" she asked.

He gazed at the rustic wood dwelling and nodded. The house belonged to Jesse, the brother he had come to meet.

Windy reached for his hand just as the front door of the house opened and a man walked out onto the porch. He stood tall, Sky noticed, broad-shouldered and muscular.

"That must be him," Sky said, thinking the man seemed too big to be called his "little" brother.

Sky helped Windy exit the car just as Jesse turned and spotted them. Even from a distance Sky saw the resemblance, the features that were his own yet different.

They faced each other moments later, staring in silence, neither it seemed, sure of what to do or say. Jesse's eyes were the color Sky remembered, a metallic shade of gray. And his hair, black as night, fell to his shoulders.

Sky took a deep breath. He had learned from a telephone conversation that Jesse was still a Hawk. The adoption had fallen through, leaving two-year-old Jesse a ward of the state, a foster child.

But there was nothing boyish about Jesse Hawk now, Sky decided, even though he was once the toddler who had lost his teddy bear.

Sky lifted the tattered animal he had felt compelled to bring. "I saved this for you," he said, glancing quickly at Windy for reassurance. She stood nearby with tears in her eyes.

Jesse took the stuffed bear and stroked its lopsided head, studying his childhood toy carefully. "I don't remember it. I suppose I was too young." He lifted his gaze and smiled, flashing a set of straight, white teeth. "But I've imagined this moment for years, wondering what you'd look like and what we'd say to each other."

Sky grinned. "I guess you never figured on me giving you a teddy bear."

"No, but I'm glad you did."

Both men looked at the tired little toy and laughed, then moved forward for a quick embrace.

When they separated, Sky stepped closer to Windy, drawing her into the meeting.

Jesse turned toward her with a welcoming smile. "Hi. You must be Windy."

She extended her hand, but Jesse reached forward and hugged her instead. A second later both he and Windy were laughing. "The baby kicked him," she told Sky.

A warm wind swirled around them, and Sky felt a sense of magic. His wife, their child, and his brother. Family.

He watched as Jesse placed his palm on Windy's belly, apparently hoping for another friendly jab. Jesse was a veterinarian, a healer of God's creatures. It seemed natural for him to touch Windy's tummy, Sky thought. He had big, strong hands, yet from the smile on Windy's face, gentle and soothing.

"You must be proud," Jesse said to Sky. "A beautiful wife and a baby on the way."

"I am," Sky responded as they stood facing each other once again, connecting like old friends. Or new relatives. The hug they'd shared had felt right—strong and brotherly.

Jesse motioned with the teddy bear. "Come on, I'll show you the house. I just bought it—haven't actually moved in yet, but it's a great old place."

Sky and Windy followed him onto the porch, but before they reached the door, Sky glanced up at the clouds. A hawk, its impressive wings spread, glided over a treetop.

"It's a red-tail," Jesse said. "A male. He's protecting the nest."

Sky smiled. He couldn't see the nest, but instinctively he knew the hawk's mate was there mothering the eggs that would soon hatch. Baby hawks—fluffy little birds—tiny messengers as sweet as the babe in Windy's womb.

Sky stood between his gentle wife and his broad-shouldered brother, thanking the heavens. The message was as clear and beautiful as this spring day. Skyler Hawk had a family now, loved ones to cherish for the rest of his life. Happiness, he knew, was his to keep.

Jesse opened the door and, as they entered the house, Sky glanced back at the tree. The red-tailed hawk had joined its mate, settling quietly into its nest.

*   *   *   *   *

Silhouette Stars

Born this month

Donald Pleasance, Alice Cooper, Mia Farrow, Burt Reynolds, Peter Gabriel, John McEnroe, Yoko Ono, Ivana Trump, Tom Courtenay, Elizabeth Taylor.

Star of the Month

Aquarius

The year ahead holds great promise. You may have to make some difficult choices early on but as the year progresses the way ahead will seem very clear. An unexpected encounter could lead to a new romance bringing the promise of future stability into your life.

SILH/HR/0201a

Pisces

You could be feeling confused over your long term plans. Get your mind off your problems, try a makeover, change your diet and take some exercise to feel more positive again.

Aries

Reckless moments could lead to some embarrassment and you may need to eat some humble pie to get a relationship back on track. A lucky win lifts your spirits.

 Taurus

Romantically a brilliant month lifting your spirits and self esteem. Any difficulties will be on the work front where someone may be jealous of your new-found confidence.

Gemini

Last month's appraisal should start to pay dividends as you feel confident that the choices you made were the right ones. A night with someone special proves to be unexpectedly passionate.

 Cancer

Time to start planning for a much needed holiday. By getting your mind off your problems and refocusing you will restore your flagging energy levels and end the month feeling happier.

Leo

Career moves are uppermost in your mind and you need to think carefully about how they could affect your personal life. An invitation brings old friends back into your life.

SILH/HR/0201c

Virgo

You need to consider a realistic financial budget to allow yourself the funds for the plans you have. Take care with how you handle a friend who is in need of your support.

Libra

You may feel frustrated by red tape or authority but keep trying as by midmonth the constraints that have held you should weaken. Late in the month there may be reason to celebrate.

Scorpio

Popular is your middle name - everyone wants a piece of you and it will be difficult to accept all the invitations. Late in the month you receive news that may lead to a change of address.

Sagittarius

You are full of ambition and there is little you can't achieve this month. Career opportunities abound and while your home life may suffer a little the rewards will more than compensate for this.

Capricorn

Whilst those around are doing their best to keep you focused at home your thoughts are fixed on more distant horizons. Finding out just how far you can go may lead to some turbulence in your life.

**Look out for more
Silhouette Stars next month**

FREE!

2 Books
and a surprise gift!

We would like to take this opportunity to thank you for reading this Silhouette® book by offering you the chance to take TWO more specially selected titles from the Desire™ series absolutely FREE! We're also making this offer to introduce you to the benefits of the Reader Service™—

- ★ FREE home delivery
- ★ FREE gifts and competitions
- ★ FREE monthly Newsletter
- ★ Books available before they're in the shops
- ★ Exclusive Reader Service discounts

Accepting these FREE books and gift places you under no obligation to buy; you may cancel at any time, even after receiving your free shipment. Simply complete your details below and return the entire page to the address below. *You don't even need a stamp!*

YES! Please send me 2 free Desire books and a surprise gift. I understand that unless you hear from me, I will receive 4 superb new titles every month for just £2.80 each, postage and packing free. I am under no obligation to purchase any books and may cancel my subscription at any time. The free books and gift will be mine to keep in any case.

DIZEB

Ms/Mrs/Miss/Mr ....Initials ....
BLOCK CAPITALS PLEASE

Surname ....

Address ....

....

....Postcode ....

Send this whole page to:
UK: The Reader Service, FREEPOST CN81, Croydon, CR9 3WZ
EIRE: The Reader Service, PO Box 4546, Kilcock, County Kildare (stamp required)